THE DYING ANIMAL

Philip Roth has won America's four major literary awards in the last decade. *Patrimony* won the 1991 National Book Critics Circle Award, *Operation Shylock* the 1993 PEN/Faulkner Award, *Sabbath's Theater* the 1995 National Book Award, and *American Pastoral* received the 1998 Pulitzer Prize in fiction.

Philip Roth was born in Newark, New Jersey, in 1933. He was educated at Bucknell University and the University of Chicago. Since 1972 he has lived in Connecticut.

ALSO BY PHILIP ROTH

Philip Roth

THE DYING ANIMAL

V

VINTAGE

Published by Vintage 2002

2 4 6 8 10 9 7 5 3 1

First published in Great Britain by
Jonathan Cape 2001

Vintage
Random House, 20 Vauxhall Bridge Road,
London SW1V 2SA

Random House Australia (Pty) Limited
20 Alfred Street, Milsons Point, Sydney
New South Wales 2061, Australia

Random House New Zealand Limited
18 Poland Road, Glenfield,
Auckland 10, New Zealand

Random House (Pty) Limited
Endulini, 5A Jubilee Road, Parktown 2193,
South Africa

The Random House Group Limited Reg. No. 954009
www.randomhouse.co.uk

A CIP catalogue record for this book
is available from the British Library

ISBN 0 09 942269 7

Papers used by Random House are natural, recyclable
products made from wood grown in sustainable forests.
The manufacturing processes conform to the environ-
mental regulations of the country of origin

Printed and bound in Great Britain by
Bookmarque Ltd, Croydon, Surrey

For N. M.

The body contains the life story just as much as the brain.

—EDNA O'BRIEN

The Dying Animal

I KNEW HER eight years ago. She was in my class. I don't teach full-time anymore, strictly speaking don't teach literature at all—for years now just the one class, a big senior seminar in critical writing called Practical Criticism. I attract a lot of female students. For two reasons. Because it's a subject with an alluring combination of intellectual glamour and journalistic glamour and because they've heard me on NPR reviewing books or seen me on Thirteen talking about culture. Over the past fifteen years, being cultural critic on the television program has made me fairly well known locally, and they're attracted to my class because of that. In the beginning, I didn't realize that talking on TV once a week for ten minutes could be so impressive as it turns out to be to these students. But they are helplessly drawn to celebrity, however inconsiderable mine may be.

Now, I'm very vulnerable to female beauty, as you know. Everybody's defenseless against something, and that's it for me. I see it and it blinds me to everything else. They come to my first class, and I know almost immediately which is the girl for me. There is a Mark Twain story in which he runs from a bull, and the bull looks up to him when he's hiding in a tree, and the bull thinks, "You are my meat, sir." Well, that "sir" is transformed into "young lady" when I see them in class. It is now eight years ago—I was already sixty-two, and the girl, who is called Consuela Castillo, was twenty-four. She is not like the rest of the class. She doesn't look like a student, at least not like an ordinary student. She's not a demi-adolescent, she's not a slouching, unkempt, "like"-ridden girl. She's well spoken, sober, her posture is perfect—she appears to know something about adult life along with how to sit, stand, and walk. As soon as you enter the class, you see that this girl either knows more or wants to. The way she dresses. It isn't exactly what's called chic, she's certainly not flamboyant, but, to begin with, she's never in jeans, pressed or unpressed. She dresses carefully, with quiet taste, in skirts, dresses, and tailored pants. Not to desensualize herself but more, it would seem, to professionalize herself, she dresses like an attractive secretary in a prestigious legal firm. Like the secretary to the bank chairman. She has a cream-colored silk blouse under a tailored blue blazer with gold buttons, a brown pocketbook with the patina of expensive leather, and little ankle boots to match, and she wears a slightly stretchy gray knitted skirt that reveals her body lines as subtly as such a skirt possibly could. Her hair is done in a natural but cared-for manner. She has a pale complexion, the mouth is bowlike though the lips are full, and she has a rounded forehead, a polished forehead of a smooth Brancusi elegance. She is Cuban. Her family are prosperous Cubans living in Jersey, across the river in Bergen County. She has black, black hair, glossy but ever so slightly coarse. And she's big. She's a big woman. The silk blouse is unbuttoned to the third button, and so you see she has powerful, beautiful breasts. You see the cleavage immediately. And you see she knows it. You see, despite the decorum, the meticulousness, the cautiously soigné style—or because of them—that she's aware of herself. She comes to the first class with the jacket buttoned over her blouse, yet some five minutes into the session, she has taken it off. When I glance her way again, I see that she's put it back on. So you understand that she's aware of her power but that she isn't sure yet how to use it, what to do with it, how much she even wants it. That body is still new to her, she's still trying it out, thinking it through, a bit like a kid walking the streets with a loaded gun and deciding whether he's packing it to protect himself or to begin a life of crime.

And she's aware of something else, and this I couldn't know from the one class meeting: she finds culture important in a reverential, old-fashioned way. Not that it's something she wishes to live by. She doesn't and she couldn't—too traditionally well brought up for that—but it's important and wonderful as nothing else she knows is. She's the one who finds the Impressionists ravishing but must look long and hard—and always with a sense of nagging confoundment—at a Cubist Picasso, trying with all her might to get the idea. She stands there waiting for the surprising new sensation, the new thought, the new emotion, and when it won't come, ever, she chides herself for being inadequate and lacking . . . what? She chides herself for not even knowing what it is she lacks. Art that smacks of modernity leaves her not merely puzzled but disappointed in herself. She would love for Picasso to matter more, perhaps to transform her, but there's a scrim drawn across the proscenium of genius that obscures her vision and keeps her worshiping at a bit of a distance. She gives to art, to all of art, far more than she gets back, a sort of earnestness that isn't without its poignant appeal. A good heart, a lovely face, a gaze at once inviting and removed, gorgeous breasts, and so newly hatched as a woman that to find fragments of broken shell adhering to that ovoid forehead wouldn't have been a surprise. I saw right away that this was going to be my girl.

Now, I have one set rule of some fifteen years' standing that I never break. I don't any longer get in touch with them on a private basis until they've completed their final exam and received their grade and I am no longer officially in loco parentis. In spite of temptation—or even a clear-cut signal to begin the flirtation and make the approach—I haven't broken this rule since, back in the mid-eighties, the phone number of the sexual harassment hotline was first posted outside my office door. I don't get in touch with them any earlier so as not to run afoul of those in the university who, if they could, would seriously impede my enjoyment of life.

I teach each year for fourteen weeks, and during that time I don't have affairs with them. I play a trick instead. It's an honest trick, it's an open and above-board trick, but it is a trick nonetheless. After the final examination and once the grades are in, I throw a party in my apartment for the students. It is always a success and it is always the same. I invite them for a drink at about six o'clock. I say that from six to eight we are going to have a drink, and they always stay till two in the morning. The bravest ones, after ten o'clock, develop into lively characters and tell me what they really are interested in. In the Practical Criticism seminar there are about twenty students, sometimes as many as twenty-five, so there will be fifteen, sixteen girls and five or six boys, of whom two or three are straight. Half of this group has left the party by ten. Generally, one straight boy, maybe one gay boy, and some nine girls will stay. They're invariably the most cultivated, intelligent, and spirited of the lot. They talk about what they're reading, what they're listening to, what art shows they've seen—enthusiasms that they don't normally go on about with their elders or necessarily with their friends. They find one another in my class. And they find me. During the party they suddenly see I am a human being. I'm not their teacher, I'm not my reputation, I'm not their parent. I have a pleasant, orderly duplex apartment, they see my large library, aisles of double-faced bookshelves that house a lifetime's reading and take up almost the entire downstairs floor, they see my piano, they see my devotion to what I do, and they stay.

My funniest student one year was like the goat in the fairy tale that goes into the clock to hide. I threw the last of them out at two in the morning, and while saying good night, I missed one girl. I said, "Where is our class clown, Prospero's daughter?" "Oh, I think Miranda left," somebody said. I went back into the apartment to start cleaning the place up and I heard a door being closed upstairs. A bathroom door. And Miranda came down the stairs, laughing, radiant with a kind of goofy abandon—I'd never, till that moment, realized that she was so pretty—and she said, "Wasn't that clever of me? I've been hiding in your upstairs bathroom, and now I'm going to sleep with you."

A little thing, maybe five foot one, and she pulled off her sweater and showed me her tits, revealing the adolescent torso of an incipiently transgressive Balthus virgin, and of course we slept together. All evening long, much like a young girl escaped from the perilous melodrama of a Balthus painting into the fun of the class party, Miranda had been on all fours on the floor with her rump raised or lying helplessly prostrate on my sofa or lounging gleefully across the arms of an easy chair seemingly oblivious of the fact that with her skirt riding up her thighs and her legs undecorously parted she had the Balthusian air of being half undressed while fully clothed. Everything's hidden and nothing's concealed. Many of these girls have been having sex since they were fourteen, and by their twenties there are one or two curious to do it with a man of my years, if just the once, and eager the next day to tell all their friends, who crinkle up their faces and ask, "But what about his skin? Didn't he smell funny? What about his long white hair? What about his wattle? What about his little pot belly? Didn't you feel sick?"

Miranda told me afterward, "You must have slept with hundreds of women. I wanted to see what it would be like." "And?" And then she said things I didn't entirely believe, but it didn't matter. She had been audacious—she had seen she could do it, game and terrified though she may have been while hiding in the bathroom. She discovered how courageous she was confronting this unfamiliar juxtaposition, that she could conquer her initial fears and any initial revulsion, and I—as regards the juxtaposition—had a wonderful time altogether. Sprawling, clowning, cavorting Miranda, posing with her underwear at her feet. Just the pleasure of looking was lovely. Though that was hardly the only reward. The decades since the sixties have done a remarkable job of completing the sexual revolution. This is a generation of astonishing fellators. There's been nothing like them ever before among their class of young women.

Consuela Castillo. I saw her and was tremendously impressed by her comportment. She knew what her body was worth. She knew what she was. She knew too she could never fit into the cultural world I lived in—culture was to bedazzle her but not something to live with. So she came to the party—beforehand I'd worried that she might not show up—and was outgoing with me there for the first time. Uncertain as to just how sober and cautious she might be, I had been careful not to reveal any special interest in her during the class meetings or on the two occasions when we met in my office to go over her papers. Nor was she, in those private meetings, anything other than subdued and respectful, taking down every word I said, no matter how unimportant. Always, in my office, she entered and exited with the tailored jacket worn over her blouse. The first time she came to see me—and we sat side by side at my desk, as directed, with the door wide open to the public corridor, all eight of our limbs, our two contrasting torsos visible to every Big Brother of a passerby (and with the window wide open as well, opened by me, flung open, for fear of her perfume)—the first time she wore elegant gray flannel cuffed pants, and the second time a black jersey skirt and black tights, but, as in class, there was always the blouse, against her white-white skin the silk blouse of one creamy shade or another unbuttoned down to the third button. At the party, however, she removed the jacket after a single glass of wine and boldly jacketless was beaming at me, offering a tantalizingly open smile. We were standing inches apart in my study, where I had been showing her a Kafka manuscript I own— three pages in Kafka's handwriting, a speech he'd given at a retirement party for the chief of the insurance office where he was working, a gift, this 1910 manuscript, from a wealthy married woman of thirty who'd been a student-mistress some years back.

Consuela was talking excitedly about everything. Letting her hold the Kafka manuscript had thrilled her, and so everything was emerging at once, questions nursed by her over that whole semester while I had secretly nursed my longing. "What music do you listen to? Do you really play the piano? Do you read all day long? Do you know all the poetry on your shelves by heart?" From every question it was clear how much she marveled—her word—at what my life was, my coherent, composed cultural life. I asked her what she was doing, what her life was like, and she told me that after high school, she didn't start college immediately—she'd decided to become a private secretary. And that's what I'd seen right off: the decorous, loyal private secretary, the office treasure to a man of power, the head of the bank or the law firm. She truly was of a bygone era, a throwback to a more mannerly time, and I guessed that her way of thinking about herself, like her way of comporting herself, had a lot to do with her being the daughter of wealthy Cuban émigrés, rich people who'd fled the revolution.

She told me, "I didn't like being a secretary. I tried it for a couple of years, but it's a dull world, and my parents always wanted and expected me to go to college. I finally decided to study instead. I suppose I was trying to be rebellious, but that was childish and so I enrolled here. I marvel at the arts." Again "marvel," used freely and sincerely. "Yes, what do you like?" I asked. "The theater. All kinds of theater. I go to the opera. My father loves the opera and we go to the Met together. Puccini's his favorite. I always love going with him." "You love your parents." "Very much," she said. "Tell me about them."

"Well, they're Cuban. Very proud. And they've done very well here. The Cubans who came here because of the revolution had a way of seeing the world so that somehow they all did extremely well. That first group, like my family, worked hard, did whatever they needed to do, did well to the point where, my grandfather used to tell us, some of them who needed public assistance when they first arrived, because they had nothing—from some of them, after a few years, the U.S. government started to receive checks paying them back. They didn't know what to do with it, my grandfather said. The first time in the history of the U.S. Treasury that they'd gotten a check back." "You love your grandfather, too. What is he like?" I asked. "Like my father—a steady person, extremely traditional, someone with an Old World view. Hard work and education first. Above everything. And like my father, very much a family man. Very religious. Though he doesn't go to church that much. Neither does my father. But my mother does. My grandmother does. My grandmother will pray the rosary every night. People bring her rosaries for presents. She has her favorites. She loves her rosary." "Do you go to church?" "When I was little. But now, no. My family is adaptable. Cubans of that generation had to be adaptable, to a degree. My family would like for us to go, my brother and me, but no, I don't." "What kind of restraints did a Cuban girl growing up in America have that wouldn't be typical of an American upbringing?" "Oh, I had a lot earlier curfew. Had to be home when all my friends were just starting to get together on a summer night. Home at eight on a summer night when I was fourteen and fifteen. But my father wasn't some frightening guy. He's just your average nice-guy dad. Except no boy was ever allowed in my room. Ever. Otherwise, when I got to be sixteen, I was treated the way my friends were being treated, in terms of curfews and stuff." "And your mother and father, when did they come here?" "In 1960. Fidel was still letting people go then. They were married in Cuba. They came to Mexico first. Then to here. I was born here, of course." "Do you think of yourself as American?" "I was born here, but, no, I'm Cuban. Very much so." "I'm surprised, Consuela. Your voice, your manner, the way you say 'stuff' and 'guy.' You're totally American to me. Why do you think of yourself as a Cuban?" "I come from a Cuban family. That's it. That's the whole story. My family has this extraordinary pride. They just love their country. It's in their hearts. It's in their blood. They were like that in Cuba." "What do they love about Cuba?" "Oh, it was so much fun. It was a society of people that had the best of all the world. Entirely cosmopolitan, especially if you lived in Havana. And it was beautiful. And they had all these great parties. It was a really good time." "Parties? Tell me about the parties." "I have these pictures of my mother at these costume balls. From the time she came out. Pictures of her at her coming-out ball." "What did her family do?" "Well, that's a long story." "Tell me." "Well, the first Spanish on my grandmother's side was sent there as a general. There was always a lot of old Spanish money. My grandmother had tutors at home, she went to Paris at eighteen to buy dresses. In my family, on both sides, there are Spanish titles. Some of them are very, very old titles. Like my grandmother is a duchess—in Spain." "And are you a duchess as well, Consuela?" "No," she said, smiling, "just a lucky Cuban girl." "Well, you could pass for a duchess. There must a duchess looking like you on the walls of the Prado. Do you know the famous painting of Velázquez, *The Maids of Honor*? Though there the little princess is fair, is blond." "I don't think I do." "It's in Madrid. In the Prado. I'll show it to you."

We went down the spiral steel staircase to my library stacks, and I found a large book of Velázquez reproductions, and we sat side by side and turned the pages for fifteen minutes, a stirring quarter hour in which we both learned something—she, for the first time, about Velázquez, and I, anew, about the delightful imbecility of lust. All this talk! I show her Kafka, Velázquez . . . why does one do this? Well, you have to do something. These are the veils of the dance. Don't confuse it with seduction. This is not seduction. What you're disguising is the thing that got you there, the pure lust. The veils veil the blind drive. Talking this talk, you have a misguided sense, as does she, that you know what you're dealing with. But it's not as though you're interviewing a lawyer or hiring a doctor and that whatever's said along the way is going to change your course of action. You know you want it and you know you're going to do it and nothing is going to stop you. Nothing is going to be said here that's going to change anything.

The great biological joke on people is that you are intimate before you know anything about the other person. In the initial moment you understand everything. You are drawn to each other's surface initially, but you also intuit the fullest dimension. And the attraction doesn't have to be equivalent: she's attracted to one thing, you to the other. It's surface, it's curiosity, but then, boom, the dimension. It's nice that she's from Cuba, it's nice that her grandmother was this and her grandfather was that, it's nice that I play the piano and own a Kafka manuscript, but all this is merely a detour on the way to getting where we're going. It's part of the enchantment, I suppose, but it's the part that if I could have none of, I'd feel much better. Sex is all the enchantment required. Do men find women so enchanting once the sex is taken out? Does anyone find anyone of any sex that enchanting unless they have sexual business with them? Who else are you that enchanted by? Nobody.

She thinks, I'm telling him who I am. He's interested in who I am. That is true, but I am curious about who she is because I want to fuck her. I don't need all of this great interest in Kafka and Velázquez. Having this conversation with her, I am thinking, How much more am I going to have to go through? Three hours? Four? Will I go as far as eight hours? Twenty minutes into the veiling and already I'm wondering, What does any of this have to do with her tits and her skin and how she carries herself? The French art of being flirtatious is of no interest to me. The savage urge is. No, this is not seduction. This is comedy. It is the comedy of creating a connection that is not the connection—that cannot begin to compete with the connection—created unartificially by lust. This is the instant conventionalizing, the giving us something in common on the spot, the trying to transform lust into something socially appropriate. Yet it's the radical inappropriateness that makes lust *lust*. No, this just plots the course, not forward but back to the elemental drive. Don't confuse the veiling with the business at hand. Sure, something else might develop, but that something has nothing to do with shopping for curtains and duvet covers and signing on as a member of the evolutionary team. The evolutionary system can work without me. I want to fuck this girl, and yes, I'll have to put up with some sort of veiling, but it's a means to an end. How much of this is cunning? I'd like to think that all of it is.

"Shall we go together to the theater sometime?" I asked her. "Oh, I'd love to do that," she said, and I didn't know then whether she was alone or had a boyfriend, but I didn't care, and two or three days later—this is all eight years back, in 1992—she wrote a note saying "It was great to be invited to the party, to see your wonderful apartment, your amazing library, to hold in my own hands the handwriting of Franz Kafka. You so generously introduced me to Diego Velázquez . . ." She included her phone number along with her address, and so I called and proposed an evening out. "Why don't you join me to go to the theater? You know what my work is. I have to go to the theater almost every week, I always have two tickets, and perhaps you'd like to come."

So we had dinner together in midtown, we went to the play, it wasn't at all interesting, and I was sitting next to her, glancing at her beautiful cleavage and her beautiful body. She has a D cup, this duchess, really big, beautiful breasts, and skin of a very white color, skin that, the moment you see it, makes you want to lick it. At the theater, in the dark, the potency of her stillness was enormous. What could be more erotic in that situation than the seeming absence in the exciting woman of any erotic intention?

After the play I said we could go for a drink, but there was one disadvantage. "People recognize me because of the television and, wherever we go, the Algonquin, the Carlyle, wherever, they may interfere with our sense of privacy." She said, "I noticed people noticing us already, at the restaurant and at the theater." "Did you mind?" I asked. "I don't know if I minded. I just noticed it. I wondered if *you* minded." "There's nothing much to be done about it," I said, "it comes with the job." "I suppose," she said, "they thought I was a groupie." "You're decidedly not a groupie," I assured her. "But I'm sure that's what they thought. 'There's David Kepesh with one of his little groupies.' They're thinking I'm some silly overwhelmed girl." "And if they did think that?" I asked. "I don't know if I like that so much. I'd like to graduate college before my parents find their daughter on Page Six of the *Post*." "I don't think you're going to be on Page Six. That's not going to happen." "I truly hope not," she said. "Look, if this is what's bothering you," I said, "we can circumvent the problem by going to my place. We can go to my apartment. We can have a drink there." "Okay," she said, but only after a serious, quietly thoughtful moment, "that's probably a better idea." Not a good idea, just a better idea.

We went to my apartment and she asked me to put on some music. I generally played easy classical music for her. Haydn trios, the *Musical Offering*, dynamic movements from the Beethoven symphonies, adagio movements from Brahms. She particularly liked Beethoven's Seventh, and on succeeding evenings she sometimes would yield to the irresistible urge to stand and move her arms playfully about in the air, as though it were she and not Bernstein conducting. Watching her breasts shift beneath her blouse while she pretended, somewhat like a performing child, to lead the orchestra with her invisible baton was intensely arousing, and, for all I know, maybe there was nothing the least bit childish about it and to excite me by way of the mock conducting was why she did it. Because it couldn't have been long before it dawned on her that to continue to believe, like a youthful student, that it was the elderly teacher who was in charge did not accord with the facts. Because in sex there is no point of absolute stasis. There is no sexual equality and there can be no sexual equality, certainly not one where the allotments are equal, the male quotient and the female quotient in perfect balance. There's no way to negotiate metrically this wild thing. It's not fifty-fifty like a business transaction. It's the chaos of eros we're talking about, the radical destabilization that is its excitement. You're back in the woods with sex. You're back in the bog. What it is is trading dominance, perpetual *imbalance*. You're going to rule out dominance? You're going to rule out yielding? The dominating is the flint, it strikes the spark, it sets it going. Then what? Listen. You'll see. You'll see what dominating leads to. You'll see what yielding leads to.

I would sometimes, as I did that night, play a Dvořák string quintet for her—electrifying music, easy enough to recognize and to grasp. She liked me to play the piano, it created a romantic, seductive atmosphere that she liked, and so I did. The simpler Chopin preludes. Schubert, some of the *Moments Musicaux*. Some movements of the sonatas. Nothing too hard, but pieces I'd studied and didn't play too badly. Usually I play only for myself, even now that I'm better at it, but it was pleasant then to play for her. It was all part of the intoxication—for both of us. Playing music is very funny. Some things come readily now, but most pieces still have a stretch that's trouble for me, passages that I never bothered to solve all those years when I was playing by myself and didn't have a teacher. When I ran into a problem back then, I figured out some nutty way to solve it. Or didn't solve it—certain types of leaps, movement from one part of the keyboard to another in an intricate way, that was kind of finger-breaking. I didn't yet have a teacher when I knew Consuela, so I did all those stupid improvised things that I invented as solutions to technical problems. I'd had only a few lessons as a kid and, until I got a teacher five years ago, I was mostly self-taught. Very little training. If I had seriously had lessons, I would spend less time practicing than I do today. I get up early and spend two, if I can two and a half hours at daybreak practicing, which is about as much as one can do. Though some days when I'm working toward something, I have another session later on. I'm in good shape, but I get tired after a while. Both mentally and physically. I have a huge amount of music that I've read through. That's a technical term—it doesn't mean looking at it like you look at a book, it means at the piano. I've bought a lot of music, I have everything, piano literature, and I used to read it, and I used to play it, badly. Some passages maybe not so badly. To see how it worked and so on. It wasn't good in terms of playing, but I had some pleasure. And pleasure is our subject. How to be serious over a lifetime about one's modest, private pleasures.

The lessons were a present to myself on my sixty-fifth birthday for finally getting over Consuela. And I've made a lot of progress. I play some pretty difficult pieces. Brahms intermezzi. Schumann. A difficult Chopin prelude. I chew a bit off a very hard one, and I still don't play it well, but I work on it. When I say to my teacher in exasperation, "I can't do it right. How do you solve this problem?" she says, "Play it a thousand times." Like all enjoyable things, you see, it has unenjoyable parts to it, but my relationship to music has deepened and that's essential to my life now. It's wise to do this now. How much longer can there possibly be girls?

I can't say that my making music excited Consuela about me the way her conducting Beethoven in jest excited me about her. I still can't say that anything I ever did sexually excited Consuela about me. Which was largely why, from the evening we first went to bed eight years back, I never had a moment's peace, why, whether she realized it or not, I was all weakness and worry from then on, why I could never figure out whether the answer was to see more of her or to see less of her or to see her not at all, to give her up—to do the unthinkable and, at sixty-two, voluntarily relinquish a gorgeous girl of twenty-four who hundreds of times said to me, "I adore you," but who never, even insincerely, could bring herself to whisper, "I desire you, I want you so—I cannot live without your cock."

That was not Consuela. Yet that was why the fear of losing her to someone else never left me, why she was continually on my mind, why with her or apart from her I never felt sure of her. The obsessional side of it was awful. When you're beguiled it helps not to think too much and just to let yourself enjoy the beguilement. But I had no such pleasure: all I did was think—think, worry, and, yes, suffer. Concentrate on your pleasure, I told myself. Why but for the pleasure do I choose to live as I do, imposing as few constraints on my independence as possible? I had the one marriage, in my twenties the bad first marriage that so many have, the bad first marriage that is as bad as boot camp, but after that I was determined not to have the bad second marriage or the third and the fourth. I was determined, after that, never to live in the cage again.

That first night we were sitting on the sofa listening to Dvořák. At one point Consuela found a book that interested her—I forget which one, though I'll never forget the moment. She turned around—I was sitting where you are, at the corner of the sofa, and she was sitting there—and she twisted her torso half around, and with the book resting on the arm of the sofa, she started to read, and because of the leaning, the bending forward, under her clothing I saw her buttocks, saw the shape clearly, which was one whopping invitation. She is a tall young woman in a slightly too narrow body. It is as if the body doesn't quite fit. Not because she's too fat. But she's by no means the anorexic type. You see there female flesh, and it is good flesh, abundant—that's *why* you see it. So there she was, not openly lying across the sofa but, all the same, with her buttocks sort of half turned to me. A woman as conscious of her body as Consuela and doing that is, I concluded, inviting me to begin. The sexual instinct is still intact—none of the Cuban correctitude has interfered. In that half-turned ass, I see that nothing has gotten in the way of the pure thing. All that we'd talked about, all that I'd had to listen to about her family, none of it has interfered. She knows how to turn her ass despite all that. Turns in the primordial way. In display. And the display is perfect. It tells me that I need no longer suppress the wish to touch.

I started to caress her buttocks, and she liked it. She said, "This is a strange situation. I can never be your girlfriend. For every possible reason. You live in a different world." "Different?" I laughed. "How different?" And right there, of course, you start the lying, and you say, "Oh, it's not such a lofty place, if that's what you're imagining. It's not such a glamorous world. It's not even a world. Once a week I appear on TV. Once a week I'm on the radio. Every few weeks I appear in print in the back pages of a magazine read by twenty people at most. My program? It's a Sunday morning cultural program. Nobody watches. It's not much of a world to worry about. I can bring you into that world easily enough. Please stay with me."

She looks to be thinking about what I've said, but what sort of thinking can it be? "Okay," she says, "for now. For tonight. But I can never be your wife." "Agreed," I said, but I thought, Who was asking her to be my wife? Who raised the question? I am sixty-two and she's twenty-four. I merely touch her ass and she tells me she can't be my wife? I didn't know such girls continued to exist. She is even more traditional than I imagined. Or maybe more odd, more unusual than I imagined. As I would discover, Consuela is ordinary but without being predictable. Nothing mechanical about her behavior. She's at once specific and mysterious, and strangely full of little surprises. But, in the beginning especially, she was difficult for me to decipher, and, mistakenly—or perhaps not—I chalked that up to her Cubanness. "I love my cozy Cuban world," she told me. "I love the coziness of my family, and I can tell already that's not something you like or want. So I never can really belong to you."

This naive niceness in combination with her marvelous body was so enticing to me that I wasn't sure even then, on that first night, that I could fuck her as though she were another cavorting Miranda. No, Consuela was not the goat in the clock. It didn't matter what she was saying—she was so damned attractive that not only could I not resist her but I didn't see how any other man could, and it was in that moment, caressing her buttocks while she explained that she could not be my wife, that my terrible jealousy was born.

The jealousy. The uncertainty. The fear of losing her, even while on top of her. Obsessions that in all my varied experience I had never known before. With Consuela as with no one else, the siphoning off of confidence was almost instantaneous.

So we went to bed. It happened fast, less because of my intoxication than because of her lack of complexity. Or call it clarity. Call it newly minted maturity, though maturity, I would say, of a simple kind: she was in communion with that body in the very way she wished and wasn't able to be in communion with art. She undressed, and not only was her blouse silk but her underwear was made of silk. She had nearly pornographic underwear. A surprise. You know she has chosen this to please. You know she has chosen this with a man's eye in mind, even if a man were never to see it. You know that you have no idea what she is, how clever she is or how stupid she is, how shallow she is or how deep she is, how innocent she is or how guileful she is, how wily, how wise, even how wicked. With a self-contained woman of such sexual power, you have no idea and you never will. The tangle that is her character is obscured by her beauty. Nonetheless, I was greatly moved by seeing that underwear. I was moved by seeing that body. "Look at you," I said.

There are two things you notice about Consuela's body. In the first place, the breasts. The most gorgeous breasts I have ever seen—and I was born, remember, in 1930: I have seen quite a few breasts by now. These were round, full, perfect. The type with the nipple like a saucer. Not the nipple like an udder but the big pale rosy-brown nipple that is so very stirring. The second thing was that she had sleek pubic hair. Normally it's curly. This was like Asian hair. Sleek, lying flat, and not much of it. The pubic hair is important because it returns.

Yes, I pulled back the covers and she came into my bed, Consuela Castillo, superclassically the fertile female of our mammalian species. And already, that first time, and at only twenty-four, she was willing to sit on top of me. She wasn't sure of herself once she was there, and till I tapped her arm to get her attention and slow her down, she was obliviously overenergetic, caroming about with her eyes shut, off in a child's game of her own. It was a little like her mock conducting. I suppose she was trying to give herself over completely, but she was too young for that and, hard as she tried, that's not what she achieved. However, because she knew how alluring her breasts were and she wanted me to be able to see them at their best, she'd climbed on top of me when I asked her to. And she did something rather pornographic for a first time, and this, again to my surprise, on her own initiative—played with her breasts around my prick. Leaned forward to place my prick between her breasts, for me to see it nestling there while she pressed them together with her hands. She knew how much this vision aroused me, the skin of the one on the skin of the other. I remember I said, "Do you realize that you have the most beautiful breasts I've ever seen?" And like the efficient, thorough private secretary taking a memo, or perhaps like the well-brought-up Cuban daughter, she replied, "Yes, I know that. I see how you respond to my breasts."

But mostly, in the beginning, the lovemaking was too spirited. She was trying too hard to impress her teacher. Slow down, be with me, I said. Less energy, more comprehension. You control the event with more subtlety than that. There's much to be said for crude naturalness, but not from afar like that. When she was first sucking me, she would move her head with a relentless rat-a-tat-tat rapidity—it was impossible not to come much sooner than I wanted to, but then, the instant I began coming, she abruptly stopped and received it like an open drain. I could have been coming into a wastepaper basket. No one had ever told her not to stop working then. None of the five previous boyfriends had dared to say that to her. They were too young. They were her age. They were glad to be getting what they got.

Then something happened. The bite. The bite *back*. The biting back of life. One night Consuela moved beyond the confines of her comforting, mannerly, habitual efficiency, progressed beyond the tutorial into the unknown adventure, and the turbulence of the affair began for me. This is how it happened. One night when she was stretched out beneath me on the bed, passively supine, waiting to have me separate her legs and slide in, I instead shoved a couple of pillows back of her head, propped up her head like that, angled it like that up against the headboard, and with my knees planted to either side of her and my ass centered over her, I leaned into her face and rhythmically, without letup, I fucked her mouth. I was so bored, you see, by the mechanical blow jobs that, to shock her, I kept her fixed there, kept her steady by holding her hair, by turning a twist of hair in one hand and wrapping it round my fist like a thong, like a strap, like the reins that fasten to the bit of a bridle.

Now, no woman really likes having her hair pulled. It's certain to turn a number of them on, but that doesn't mean they like it. And they don't like it because there's no way of getting around the act of domination that is going on, that must go on, that lets them think, It's just what I imagined sex to be. It *is* brutish—this guy's not a brute but he's on to the brutishness. After I came, when I drew away, Consuela looked not just horrified but ferocious. Yes, something is finally happening to her. It is no longer so comfortable for her. She is no longer practicing scales. Uncontrollably she is in motion within. I was still above her—kneeling over her and dripping on her—we were looking each other cold in the eye, when, after swallowing hard, she snapped her teeth. Suddenly. Cruelly. At me. It wasn't an act. It was instinctive. It was snapping her teeth by using the full force of the masticatory muscles to violently raise the lower jaw. It was as though she were saying, That's what I could have done, that's what I wanted to do, and that's what I didn't do.

At last the forthright, incisive, elemental response from the contained classical beauty. Till then it was all controlled by narcissism, by exhibitionism, and despite the energetic display, despite the audacity, it was strangely inert. I don't know whether Consuela remembers that bite, that activating bite that freed her from her own surveillance and inaugurated her into the sinister dream, but I will never forget it. The full amorous truth. The instinctual girl bursting not just the container of her vanity but the captivity of her cozy Cuban home. It was the true beginning of her mastery—the mastery into which my mastery had initiated her. I am the author of her mastery of me.

You see, I think that in me Consuela sensed a possessable version of her family's refinement, of that unrecoverable aristocratic past that is more or less a myth to her. A man of the world. A cultural authority. Her teacher. Now, most people are appalled by the vast difference in age, but it is the very thing Consuela is drawn to. The erotic oddness is all most people register, and they register it as repugnance, as repugnant farce. But the age I am has great significance for Consuela. These girls with old gents don't do it despite the age—they're drawn to the age, they do it *for* the age. Why? In Consuela's case, because the vast difference in age gives her permission to submit, I think. My age and my status give her, rationally, the license to surrender, and surrendering in bed is a not unpleasant sensation. But simultaneously, to give yourself over intimately to a much, much older man provides this sort of younger woman with authority of a kind she cannot get in a sexual arrangement with a younger man. She gets both the pleasures of submission *and* the pleasures of mastery. A boy submitting to her power, what does that amount to in a creature so patently desirable? But to have this man of the world submitting solely because of the force of her youth and her beauty? To have gained the total interest, to have become the consuming passion of a man inaccessible in every other arena, to enter a life she admires that would otherwise be closed to her—that's power, and it's the power she wants. It isn't that the dominance is being traded sequentially; it's being traded continuously. Not so much being traded as being braided. And therein lies the source not only of my obsession with her but of her counterobsession with me. Or so I had it figured at the time, for all the good it did me in attempting to understand what she was up to and why I was getting in deeper and deeper.

No matter how much you know, no matter how much you think, no matter how much you plot and you connive and you plan, you're not superior to sex. It's a very risky game. A man wouldn't have two-thirds of the problems he has if he didn't venture off to get fucked. It's sex that disorders our normally ordered lives. I know this as well as anyone. Every last vanity will come back to mock you. Read Byron's *Don Juan*. Yet what do you do if you're sixty-two and believe you'll never have a claim on something so perfect again? What do you do if you're sixty-two

---

and the urge to take whatever is still takable couldn't be stronger? What do you do if you're sixty-two and you realize that all those bodily parts invisible up to now (kidneys, lungs, veins, arteries, brain, intestines, prostate, heart) are about to start making themselves distressingly apparent, while the organ most conspicuous throughout your life is doomed to dwindle into insignificance?

Don't misunderstand me. It isn't that, through a Consuela, you can delude yourself into thinking that you have a last shot at your youth. You never feel the difference from youth more. In her energy, in her enthusiasm, in her youthful unknowing, in her youthful *knowing*, the difference is dramatized every moment. There's never any mistaking that it's she and not you who is twenty-four. You'd have to be a clod to feel you're young again. If you felt youthful, it would be a snap. Far from feeling youthful, you feel the poignancy of her limitless future as opposed to your own limited one, you feel even more than you ordinarily do the poignancy of every last grace that's been lost. It's like playing baseball with a bunch of twenty-year-olds. It isn't that you feel twenty because you're playing with them. You note the difference every second of the game. But at least you're not sitting on the sidelines.

Here's what happens: you feel excruciatingly how old you are, but in a new way.

Can you imagine old age? Of course you can't. I didn't. I couldn't. I had no idea what it was like. Not even a false image—no image. And nobody wants anything else. Nobody wants to face any of this before he has to. How is it all going to turn out? Obtuseness is de rigueur.

Understandably, any stage of life more advanced than one's own is unimaginable. Sometimes one is halfway through the next stage before one realizes that one has entered it. And then, earlier stages of advancement offer their compensations. And even so, the middle is daunting for many people. But the end? It is, interestingly, the first time of life that you stand entirely outside of while you're in it. Observing one's decay all the while (if one is as fortunate as I am), one has, by virtue of one's continuing vitality, considerable distance from one's decay—even feels oneself jauntily independent of it. Inevitably, yes, there is a multiplication of the signs leading to the unpleasant conclusion, and yet despite that, you stand outside. And the ferocity of the objectivity is brutal.

There's a distinction to be made between dying

and death. It's not all uninterrupted dying. If one's healthy and feeling well, it's invisible dying. The end that is a certainty is not necessarily boldly announced. No, you can't understand. The only thing you understand about the old when you're not old is that they have been stamped by their time. But understanding only that freezes them in their time, and so amounts to no understanding at all. To those not yet old, being old means *you've been*. But being old also means that despite, in addition to, and in excess of your beenness, you still are. Your beenness is very much alive. You still are, and one is as haunted by the still-being and its fullness as by the having-already-been, by the pastness. Think of old age this way: it's just an everyday fact that one's life is at stake. One cannot evade knowing what shortly awaits one. The silence that will surround one forever. Otherwise it's all the same. Otherwise one is immortal for as long as one lives.

Not too many years ago, there was a ready-made way to be old, just as there was a ready-made way to be young. Neither obtains any longer. A great fight about the permissible took place here—and a great overturning. Nonetheless, should a man of seventy still be involved in the carnal aspect of the human comedy? To be unapologetically an unmonastic old man susceptible still to the humanly exciting? That is not the condition as it was once symbolized by the pipe and the rocking chair. Maybe it's still a bit of an affront to people, to fail to abide by the old clock of life. I realize that I can't count on the virtuous regard of other adults. But what can I do about the fact that, as far as I can tell, nothing, *nothing* is put to rest, however old a man may be?

She began coming to my place in a very casual manner after that bite. It was no longer a matter of evening dates and then the fucking once she realized the little it took for her to control things. She phoned and she said, "Could I come for a few hours?" and she knew I would never say no, knew that every time, to get to hear me say "Look at you" as though she were herself a Picasso, she had merely to undress and stand there. I, her teacher in Practical Criticism, the Sunday morning PBS aesthetician, New York television's reigning authority on what is the current best to see, hear, and read—I had pronounced her a great work of art, with all the magical influence of a great work of art. Not the artist but the art itself. There was nothing for her not to understand—she had only to be there, on view, and the understanding of her importance flowed from me. It was not required of her, any more than it is of a violin concerto or of the moon, that she have any sort of self-conception. That's what I was for: I was Consuela's awareness of herself. I was the cat watching the goldfish. Only it was the goldfish that had the teeth.

The jealousy. *That* poison. And unprovoked. Jealous even when she tells me she's going ice-skating with her eighteen-year-old brother. Will he be the one who steals her away? With these obsessional love affairs you are not your own confident self, not when you're in the vortex of them and not when the girl is almost a third your age. I feel anxious unless I speak to her on the phone every day, and then I feel anxious after we've spoken. Women who in the past demanded regular calls, telephoning back and forth like that, I'd invariably gotten rid of—and now it was I demanding it of her: the daily fix by phone. Why do I flatter her when we speak? Why don't I stop telling her how perfect she is? Why do I always feel I'm saying the wrong thing to this girl? I'm unable to make out what she makes of me, what she makes of anything, and my confusion causes me to say things that sound false or exaggerated to my ear, so I hang up full of silent resentment toward her. But when the rare day passes that I'm able to discipline myself enough not to speak to her, not to call her, not to flatter her, not to sound false, not to resent what she unknowingly does to me, it's worse. I can't stop doing anything I'm doing, and everything I'm doing leaves me upset. I don't feel the authority with her that's necessary for my stability, and yet she comes to me because of that authority.

On the nights she isn't with me, I am deformed by thinking about where she may be and what she may be up to. But then even after she has been with me for the evening and has gone home, I can't sleep. The experience of her is too strong. I sit up in bed and in the middle of the night I cry out, "Consuela Castillo, leave me alone!" That's enough, I tell myself. Get up, change the sheets, shower again, get rid of the smell of her, *and then get rid of her.* You must. It's become an endless campaign with her. Where's the fulfillment and the sense of possession? If you have her, why can't you have her? You're not getting what you want even when you're getting what you want. There is no peace in it and there can't be, because of our ages and the unavoidable poignancy. Because of our ages, I have the pleasure but I never lose the longing. Had this never happened before? No. I was never sixty-two years old before. I was no longer in that phase of my life when I thought I could do everything. Yet I remembered it clearly. You see a beautiful woman. You see her from a mile away. You go to her and say, "Who are you?" You have dinner. And so on. *That* phase, when it's worry-free.

You get on the bus. A creature so gorgeous everybody is afraid to sit next to her. The seat next to the most beautiful girl in the world—and it's empty. So you take it. But now isn't then, and it'll never be calm, it'll never be peaceful. I was worried about her walking around in that blouse. Peel off her jacket, and there is the blouse. Peel off the blouse, and there is perfection. A young man will find her and take her away. And from me, who fired up her senses, who gave her her stature, who was the catalyst to her emancipation and prepared her for him.

How do I know a young man will take her away? Because I once was the young man who would have done it.

When I was younger I wasn't susceptible. Others got jealous earlier, but I was able to protect myself from that. I let them have their way, confident that I could prevail through sexual dominance. But jealousy, of course, is the trap door to the contract. Men respond to jealousy by saying, "Nobody else is going to have her. I'm going to have her—I'll marry her. I'll capture her that way. By convention." Marriage cures the jealousy. That's why many men seek it out. Because they're not sure of that other person, they get her to sign the contract: *I will not, et cetera.*

How do I capture Consuela? The thought is morally humiliating, yet there it is. I'm certainly not going to hold her by promising marriage, but how else can you hold a young woman at my age? What am I able to offer instead in this milk-and-honey society of free-market sex? And so that's when the pornography begins. The pornography of jealousy. The pornography of one's own destruction. I am rapt, I am enthralled, and yet I am enthralled *outside* the frame. What is it that puts me outside? It is age. The wound of age. Pornography in its classic form has a kick of about five or ten minutes before it becomes kind of comical. But in this pornography the images are extremely painful. Ordinary pornography is the aestheticizing of jealousy. It takes the torment out. What—why "aestheticizing"? Why not "anesthetizing"? Well, perhaps both. It's a representation, ordinary pornography. It's a fallen art form. It's not just make-believe, it's patently insincere. You want the girl in the porno film, but you're not jealous of whoever's fucking her because he becomes your surrogate. Quite amazing, but that's the power of even fallen art. He becomes a stand-in, there in your service; that removes the sting and turns it into something pleasant. Because you're an invisible accomplice in the act, ordinary pornography takes the torment out while mine keeps the torment in. In my pornography, you identify yourself not with the satiate, with the person who is getting it, but with the person not getting it, with the person losing it, with the person who has lost.

A young man will find her and take her away. I see him. I know him. I know what he is capable of doing because he is me at twenty-five, as yet without the wife and the child; he is me in the raw, before I did what everybody else did. I see him watch her crossing the broad plaza—*striding* the plaza—at Lincoln Center. He is out of sight, behind a pillar, eyeing her as I did on the evening I took her to her first Beethoven concert. She is in boots, high leather boots and a shapely short dress, a devastating young woman out in the open on a warm autumn night, unashamedly walking the streets of the world for all to covet and admire—and she's smiling. She's happy. This devastating woman is coming to meet me. Only it isn't me in the pornographic film. It's him. It's the him who was once me but is no longer. Watching him watching her, I know in detail what is going to happen next, and knowing what is going to happen next, picturing it, it is impossible to think in what you rationally construe as your own self-interest. It is impossible to think that not everybody is feeling this way about this girl because not everybody has an obsession about this girl. Instead, you can't imagine her going anywhere. You can't imagine her on the street, in a store, at a party, on the beach without that guy emerging from the shadows. The pornographic torment: watching somebody else do it who once was you.

When you finally lose a girl like Consuela, this happens to you everywhere, all the places you ever were with her. When she's gone, it's uncanny, you'll remember her there, you'll see that space empty of you but with her as she was with you but with the twenty-five-year-old boy you are no longer. You imagine her striding like that in her shapely short dress. Coming toward you. Aphrodite. Then she is past you, she's gone, and the pornography spins out of control.

I inquire (though what good can come of my knowing?) about her boyfriends, ask her to tell me how many she slept with before me and when she started and whether she's ever been with another girl or with two boys at once (or a horse, or a parrot, or a monkey), and that was when she told me that there had been only five. However attractive, however well groomed and gorgeous, she had had relatively few boyfriends for a contemporary girl. The constraining influence of the wealthy, proper Cuban background (if, that is, she is telling the truth). And the last boyfriend was a stupid fellow student who couldn't even fuck her right, who was only concentrating on coming himself. The old stupid story. Not a man who loves women.

She was inconsistent in her morality, by the way. I remember that at that time George O'Hearn, the poet, a man married to the same woman all his life, had a girlfriend in Consuela's neighborhood, and he was there, downtown, having breakfast with his girlfriend in a coffee shop, and Consuela saw him and she was upset. She recognized him from the picture on the back of a new book of his then on the table beside my bed, and she knew that I knew him. She came to me that night. "I saw your friend. He was with a girl at eight o'clock in the morning, in a restaurant, and he was kissing her—and he's married." She was so predictably platitudinous in these things while acting independently of all convention in her affair with someone thirty-eight years her senior. Inwardly uncertain and out of her depth some of the time, that had to be; nonetheless, something special was happening to her, a big, ersatz, unforeseen something that flattered her vanity and fed her confidence and, exciting as it was, didn't appear to be turning her (as it was me) inside out.

Consuela told me, during one of my interrogations, that there was a boyfriend back in high school who used to want passionately to watch her menstruate. Whenever she started to menstruate, she was to call him, and he would come right over, and she would stand there, and he would watch the blood run down her thighs and onto the floor. "You did this for him?" I asked. "Yes." "And your family, what about your traditional family? You were fifteen years old, you couldn't stay out in the summertime after eight P.M., and yet you did this? Your grandmother a duchess," I said, "in love with her rosary, and yet you did this?" "I wasn't fifteen any longer. I was sixteen by then." "Sixteen. I see. That explains it. And how often did you do this?" "Whenever I had my period. Every month," she told me. "Who was the boy? I thought a boy couldn't even be in your room. Who was he? Who *is* he?"

A socially acceptable boy. Also Cuban. Carlos Alonso. Very proper, clean-cut kid, she tells me, who picked her up at the door in a suit and a tie, never honked for her at the curb, who would come in and meet her parents and sit with them, a reserved boy from a good family highly conscious of their social status. As in her own family there is lots of respect for the father, everyone is well educated, everyone is easily bilingual, the right schools, the right country club, they read *El Diario* and the *Bergen Record*, they love Reagan, love Bush, hate Kennedy, rich New

Jersey Cubans to the right of Louis XIV, and Carlos calls her up and says don't menstruate without me.

Picture it. After school, the bathroom, suburban Bergen County, and the two of them transfixed by the enigma of her discharge as though they are Adam and Eve. Because Carlos is enchanted too. He too knows she is a work of art, the lucky rare woman who is a work of art, classical art, beauty in its classical form, but alive, alive, and the aesthetic response to beauty alive is what, class? Desire. Yes, Carlos is her mirror. Men have always been her mirror. They even want to watch her menstruate. She is the female magic men cannot escape. Dressed culturally in the decorous Cuban past, but her permissions flow from her vanity. Her permissions flow from looking in the mirror and saying, "Someone else must see this."

"Call *me*," I told her, "when you begin to menstruate. I want you to come *here*. I want to watch *too*."

Too. That's how unconcealed the jealousy is, how feverish the desire is—and that's how something close to disastrous happened.

Because I was meanwhile, that year, having an affair with a very attractive, very strong, responsible woman, no disabling wounds, no vices or wild views, a scrutinizing intelligence, reliable in every way, too unironic ever to be lightly witty but a sensual, expert, and attentive lover. Carolyn Lyons. Many years earlier, back in the mid-sixties, she'd been a student of mine as well. In the intervening decades, however, neither of us had gone in search of the other, and so when we accidentally met on the street as Carolyn was walking to work one morning, we embraced and held each other as if it were a cataclysmic event like a world war (rather than her leaving for California to go to law school) that had separated us for the next twenty-four years. We each proclaimed how wonderful the other looked, laughingly recalled the mania of a night in my office when she was nineteen, said all sorts of tender things about the past, and there and then made a date for dinner the next night.

Carolyn was still beautiful, radiantly big-featured, though beneath the pale gray eyes the biggish sockets were now papery and worn, and not so much, I would think, because of her chronic insomnia but because of that compound of disappointments not uncommon to the biographies of successful professional women in their forties whose evening meals more often than not are delivered to the door of their Manhattan apartments in a plastic bag by an immigrant. And her body took up more space than it used to. Two divorces, no children, a demanding, high-paying job requiring a lot of overseas travel—

all that adds up to another thirty-five pounds, and so when we went to bed, she whispered, "I'm not the same," to which I replied, "Do you think I am?" and nothing was said on that score again.

As an undergraduate, Carolyn had roomed with one of the campus firebrands, a charismatic sixties ringleader, à la Abbie Hoffman, named Janie Wyatt, a kid from Manhasset who wrote an enchanting senior thesis for me entitled "A Hundred Ways to Be Perverse in the Library." I quote the opening sentence: "The blow job in the library is the very essence of it, the sanctified transgression, the campus black mass." Janie weighed maybe a hundred pounds, no more than five feet tall, if that, a little blonde who looked as if you could pick her up and throw her around, and she was the college's dirty diva.

Carolyn back then was in awe of Janie. Carolyn used to say to me, "She has so many affairs. Simultaneously. You go to somebody's apartment, a graduate student, a young instructor, and there's Janie's underwear hanging out to dry on the handles of the shower faucets." Students who wanted sex, Carolyn would tell me, they'd be walking along the campus, they'd suddenly want sex, and they'd call her. And if she wanted it too, off they went. They'd be walking along, they'd stop in their tracks, they'd say, "I think

I'm just going to call Janie," and they never made it to class. A lot of the faculty frowned at the openness of her sexual behavior and equated it with stupidity. Even some of the boys—spoke of her as a slut one moment and then went off to bed with her the next. But she was neither stupid nor a slut. Janie was someone who knew what she was doing. She stood in front of you, small as she was, with her legs slightly apart, planted, lots of freckles, blond short hair, no makeup except bright red lipstick, and her big, open confessional grin: this is what I am, this is what I do, if you don't like it, it's too bad.

How did Janie astonish me most? Many ways—in the early days of the campus revolt, there were many things to mark her as a new, noteworthy kind of creature. She astonished me, strangely, by doing something that might sound nothing like immoderate now, given the progress in boldness that women have made since, and that didn't necessarily rival the defiant flamboyance of her public stance. She astonished me most by carrying off the shyest man on the campus, our poet. The crossover between faculty and students was exciting not only for being new but for being out in the open, and accounted for more divorces than just my own. The poet was without the skills others possess in advancing their worldly interests. He marshaled his egoism for language alone. Eventually died from drink, relatively young, but, on his own in genial America, only drink could unstring this guy. Married, with two kids, bashful as could be other than up on the platform dazzlingly lecturing on poetry. To lure this man out of the shadows was unimaginable. Except to Janie. At a party. Many students, both boys and girls, wanted to be closer to him. The smart girls all had a crush on him, this romantic stranger from life, but he didn't appear to trust anybody. Until Janie went up to him at a party and took his hand and said, "Let's dance," and the next thing we knew she had him in tow. He seemed to swim right in to trusting her. Little Janie Wyatt: we're all equal, we're all free, we can land anything we want.

Janie and Carolyn, along with another three or four defiant upper-middle-class kids, comprised a clique calling itself the Gutter Girls. Well, these girls resembled nothing I'd ever known, and not because they were swathed in gypsy rags and barefoot. They detested innocence. They couldn't bear supervision. They weren't afraid of being conspicuous and they weren't afraid of being clandestine. To rebel against one's condition was everything. They and their adherents may well have been, historically, the first wave of American girls fully implicated in their own desire. No rhetoric, no ideology, just the playing field of pleasure opening out to the bold. The boldness developed as they realized what the possibilities were, when they realized they were no longer being watched, that they were no longer subservient to the old system or under any system of any kind—when they realized they could do anything.

It was an improvised revolution at first, the sixties revolution; the campus vanguard was tiny, half of one percent, maybe a percent and a half, but that didn't matter because the vibrating faction of society soon followed. Culture is always being led by its narrowest point, among the young women on this campus by Janie's Gutter Girls, the female trailblazers of a completely spontaneous sexual change. Twenty years earlier, in my college days, the campuses had been perfectly managed. Parietal regulations. Unquestioned supervision. The authority came from a distant Kafkaesque source—"the administration"—and the language of the administration could have come from Saint Augustine. You tried to find your wily way around all this control, but until about '64, by and large everyone under surveillance was law-abiding, members in excellent standing of what Hawthorne called "the limit-loving class." Then came the long-delayed explosion, the disreputable assault on post-war normalcy and the cultural consensus. All that was unmanageable came breaking out, and the irreversible transformation of the young had begun.

Carolyn never achieved Janie's notoriety, nor did she want to. Carolyn partook of the protest, the provocation, the insolent fun but, with characteristic self-discipline, never to the point where insubordination might jeopardize her future. Carolyn as she is now in middle age—entirely of the corporate world, uncomplainingly straight—isn't a surprise to me. Giving offense in the cause of sexual license was never Carolyn's calling. Neither was wholesale waywardness. But Janie—let me digress for a moment to Janie, in her own small-time way a Consuela Castillo's Simón Bolívar. Yes, a great revolutionary leader like the South American Bolívar, whose armies destroyed the power of colonialist Spain—an insurrectionist unafraid of battling superior forces, the *libertador* pitted against the college's reigning morality who eventually swept its authority away.

Today, the carefree sexual conduct of the well-bred girls in my class is, as far as they know, warranted by the Declaration of Independence, an entitlement that requires of them little if any courage to utilize and that is in harmony with the pursuit of happiness as conceived of at Philadelphia in 1776. In fact, the uninhibited everything that the Consuelas and the Mirandas nonchalantly take for granted derives from the audacity of the shameless, subversive Janie Wyatts and the amazing victory they achieved in the sixties through the force of atrocious behavior. The coarse dimension of American life previously captured in gangster films, that's what Janie hauled on campus, because that's the intensity it took to undo the upholders of the norms. That's how you carried the quarrel to your keepers—in your ugly language rather than theirs.

Janie was born in the city, then raised in the suburbs, out on Long Island, in Manhasset. Her mother was a schoolteacher and commuted each day to Queens, which the family had left for Manhasset and where the mother still taught tenth grade. The father commuted in the other direction, the couple of miles to Great Neck, where he was a law partner of Carolyn's father. That's how the girls knew each other. The empty suburban house—it excites every sexual nerve in Janie's body. She comes of sexual age when the music is changing, and so she turns it on. She turns everything on. Janie's cunning was that she realized, when she got there, what the suburbs were for. She was never free in the city as a girl, never on the loose as the boys were. But out in Manhasset she found her frontier. There were next-door neighbors but they weren't as close as they were in the city. She got home from school and the streets were empty. Looked like the towns of the old Wild West. Nobody around. Everybody gone. So till they all came home on the train, she had a little operation, a little sideshow going. Thirty years later, a Janie Wyatt degenerates into an Amy Fisher, slavishly servicing the auto mechanic all on her own, but Janie was bright and a born organizer—unbroken, brazen, a sassy surfer riding the currents of change. The suburbs, where girls, safe from the dangers of the city, didn't have to be kept under tight wraps, where parents weren't too concerned on a moment-by-moment basis, the suburbs were her American finishing school. The suburbs created the agora for this education in the unsanctioned to flourish. The lessening of surveillance, the gradual giving over of space to all these kids who had been endowed by Dr. Spock with the tools of disobedience—and it flourished, all right. It grew out of control.

That was the transformation Janie wrote about in her thesis. That was the story she told. The Suburbs. The Pill. The Pill that gave parity to the woman. The Music. Little Richard propelling everything. The Pelvic Backbeat. The Car. The kids out there driving together in the Car. The Prosperity. The Commute. The Divorce. A lot of adult distraction. The Grass. Dope. Dr. Spock. All of that's what led to Lord of the Flies U, which was what the Gutter Girls called our college. Janie's was not a revolutionary cell that was blowing things up. Janie wasn't Bernadine Dohrn or Kathy Boudin. Nor were the Betty Friedans speaking to her. The Gutter Girls had no objection to the social or the political argument, but that was the other side of the decade. There were two strains to the turbulence: there was the libertarianism extending orgiastic permission to the individual and opposed to the traditional interests of the community, but with it, often wedded to it, there was the communal righteousness about civil rights and against the war, the disobedience whose moral prestige devolves through Thoreau. And the two strains interconnecting made the orgy difficult to discredit.

But Janie's was a pleasure cell, not a political cell. And these pleasure cells existed not just on our campus but all over and by the thousands, tie-dyed boys and girls who didn't always smell so good engaging together in reckless behavior. Twist and shout, work it on out—that, not the "Internationale," was their anthem. Salacious, direct music to fuck to. Music to give head by, the people's bebop. Of course, music has always been useful sexually, within the prescribed limitations of the moment. Even Glenn Miller, back when in a song you still had to come at sex through a Tin Pan Alley romance, lubricated the situation as much as it could be. Then young Sinatra. Then the creamy saxophone. But the limitations on the Gutter Girls? They used the music the way they used the marijuana, as a propulsive, as the emblem of their mutiny, the provocation to erotic vandalism. In my adolescence, in the swing band era, there was just the booze to put you in the mood. For them there was an arsenal of all-out anti-inhibitors.

Having those girls in class was my education: seeing how they got themselves up, watching them jettison their manners and uncover their crudeness, listening to their music with them, smoking with them and listening to Janis Joplin, their Bessie Smith in whiteface, their shouter, their honky-tonk, stoned Judy Garland, listening with them to Jimi Hendrix, their Charlie Parker of the guitar, getting high with them and listening to Hendrix playing the guitar backwards, reversing everything, retarding the beat, accelerating the beat, and Janie chanting, as her doped-out mantra, "Hendrix and sex, Hendrix and sex," and Carolyn, as hers, "A beautiful man with a beautiful voice"—observing the swagger and appetite and excitement of the Janies who were without the biological terror of the erection, without the fear of the phallic transformation of the man.

The Janie Wyatts of the American sixties knew how to operate around engorged men. They were themselves engorged, so they knew how to transact business with them. The venturous male drive, the male initiative, wasn't a lawless action requiring denunciation and adjudication but a sexual sign that one responds to or not. To control the male impulse and report it? They were not educated in that ideological system. They were far too playful to be indoctrinated with animus and resentment and grievance from above. They were educated in the instinctual system. They weren't interested in replacing the old inhibitions and prohibitions and moral instruction with new forms of surveillance and new systems of control and a new set of orthodox beliefs. They knew where the pleasure was to be had, and they knew how to give over to desire without fear. Unafraid of the aggressive impulse, deep in the transforming fracas—and for the first time on American soil since the Pilgrim women of Plymouth Colony were cloistered by an ecclesiastical government against the corruptions of the flesh and the sinfulness of men—a generation drawing their conclusions from their cunts about the nature of experience and the delights of the world.

Isn't the bolivar the unit of currency in Venezuela? Well, under America's first woman president, I would hope the dollar will become the wyatt. Janie deserves no less. She democratized the entitlement to pleasure.

Sidelight. The English trading outpost at Merry Mount that so incensed the Plymouth Puritans—know about that? Fur-trading settlement, smaller than Plymouth, about thirty miles northwest of Plymouth. Where Quincy, Mass., is today. Men drinking, selling arms to the Indians, palling around with the Indians. Cavorting with the enemy. Copulating with Indian women, whose custom it was to assume the doggie position and to be taken from behind. A pagan hotbed in Puritan Massachusetts, where the Bible was law. Danced around a maypole in animal masks, worshiped at it every month. Hawthorne based a story on that maypole: Governor Endicott sent the Puritan militia under Miles Standish to cut it down, a pine tree festooned with colored banners and ribbons and antlers and roses and standing eighty feet tall. "Jollity and gloom were contending for an empire"—that's how Hawthorne understood it.

Merry Mount was presided over for a time by a speculator, a lawyer, a charismatic privileged character named Thomas Morton. He's a kind of forest creature out of *As You Like It*, a wild demon out of *A Midsummer Night's Dream*. Shakespeare is Morton's contemporary, born only about eleven or so years before Morton. Shakespeare is Morton's rock-and-roll. The Plymouth Puritans busted him, then the Salem Puritans busted him—put him in the stocks, fined him, imprisoned him. He eventually exiled himself to Maine, where he died in his late sixties. But he couldn't resist provoking them. He was a source of prurient fascination for the Puritans. Because if one's piety isn't absolute, it logically leads to a Morton. The Puritans were terrified that their daughters would be carried off and corrupted by this merry miscegenator out at Merry Mount. A white man, a white Indian, luring the virgins away? This was even more sinister than red Indians stealing them. Morton was going to turn their daughters into the Gutter Girls. That was the main concern other than his trading with the Indians and selling them firearms. The Puritans were frantic about the younger generation. Because once they lost their younger generation, the ahistorical experiment in dictatorial intolerance was dead. Age-old American story: save the young from sex. Yet it's always too late. Too late because they've already been born.

Twice they shipped Morton to England to be tried for disobedience, but the English ruling class and the Church of England had no use for the New England Separatists. Morton's case was thrown out of court each time, and Morton made his way back to New England. The English thought, He's right, Morton —we wouldn't want to live with him either, but he's not coercing anyone and these fucking Puritans are crazy.

In *Of Plymouth Plantation,* Governor William Bradford's book, the governor writes amply about the evils of Merry Mount, the "riotous prodigality," the "profuse excess." "They fell to great licentiousness and led a dissolute life, pouring out themselves into all profaneness." Morton's confederates he calls "mad Bacchanalians." Morton he labels "the Lord of Misrule" and the master of "a School of Atheism." Governor Bradford's a powerful ideologue. Piety knew how to write sentences in the seventeenth century. So too did impiety. Morton published a book as well, *The New English Canaan,* grounded in fascinated observation of the Indians' society—but a scurrilous book according to Bradford, because it was also about the Puritans and how they "make a great show of religion but no humanity." Morton is straightforward. Morton doesn't expurgate. You have to wait three hundred years before the voice of Thomas Morton turns up in America again, un-expurgated, as Henry Miller. The clash between Plymouth and Merry Mount, between Bradford and Morton, between rule and misrule—the colonial harbinger of the national upheaval three hundred and thirty-odd years later when Morton's America was born at last, miscegenation and all.

No, the sixties weren't aberrant. The Wyatt girl wasn't aberrant. She was a natural Mortonian in the conflict that's been ongoing from the beginning. Out in the American wildness, order will reign. The Puritans were the agents of rule and godly virtue and right reason, and on the other side was misrule. But why is it rule and misrule? Why isn't Morton the great theologian of no-rules? Why isn't Morton seen for what he is, the founding father of personal freedom? In the Puritan theocracy you were at liberty to do good; in Morton's Merry Mount you were at liberty—that was it.

And there were lots of Mortons. Mercantile adventurers without the ideology of holiness, people who didn't give a damn whether they were elect or not. They came over with Bradford on the *May-*

flower, emigrated later on other ships, but you don't hear about them at Thanksgiving, because they couldn't stand these communities of saints and believers where no deviation was allowed. Our earliest American heroes were Morton's oppressors: Endicott, Bradford, Miles Standish. Merry Mount's been expunged from the official version because it's the story not of a virtuous utopia but of a utopia of candor. Yet it's Morton whose face should be carved in Mount Rushmore. That's going to happen too, the very day they rename the dollar the wyatt.

My Merry Mount? Me and the sixties? Well, I took seriously the disorder of those relatively few years, and I took the word of the moment, liberation, in its fullest meaning. That's when I left my wife. To be accurate, she discovered me with the Gutter Girls and she threw me out. Now, there were others on the faculty who grew their hair long and wore the far-out clothes, but they were just on furlough. They were a mix of voyeur and day-tripper. Occasionally they ventured out, but never did more than a few go over the trench into the field of engagement. But I was determined, once I saw the disorder for what it was, to seize from the moment a rationale for myself, to undo my former allegiances and my current allegiances and not to do it on the side, not to be, as many my age were, either inferior to it or superior to it or simply titillated by it, but to follow the logic of this revolution to its conclusion, and without having become its casualty.

This required some doing. Just because there's no memorial bearing the names of those who out on the rampage came to grief doesn't mean there weren't casualties. There wasn't necessarily carnage, but there was plenty of breakage. This was not a pretty revolution taking place on the dignified theoretical plane. This was a puerile, preposterous, uncontrolled, drastic mess, the whole society in a huge brawl. Though there was comedy too. It was a revolution that at the same time was like the day after the revolution—a big idyll. People took off their underwear and walked around laughing. Often it was no more than farce, childish farce, but astonishingly far-reaching childish farce; often it was no more than a teenage power surge, the adolescence of the biggest, most powerful American generation ever coming into their hormones all at once. Yet the impact was revolutionary. Things forever changed.

One's skepticism, one's cynicism, the cultural-political good sense that normally kept one outside of mass movements, was a useful shield. I wasn't as high as everyone else, and I didn't want to be. For me the job was to detach the revolution from its immediate paraphernalia, from its pathological trappings and its rhetorical inanities and the pharmacological dynamite that made people jump out of windows, to sidestep the worst and to seize and use the idea, to say to oneself, What a chance this is, what an opportunity to live out my own revolution. Why rein myself in because of the accident of the fact that I was born in this year and not in that year?

People fifteen, twenty years younger than I, the privileged beneficiaries of the revolution, could afford to go through it unconsciously. There was this exuberant party, this squalid paradise of disarray, and, without thinking or having to think, they claimed it, and usually with all its trivia and trash. But I had to think. There I was, still in the prime of life and the country entering into this extraordinary time. Am I or am I not a candidate for this wild, sloppy, raucous repudiation, this wholesale wrecking of the inhibitive past? Can I master the discipline of freedom as opposed to the recklessness of freedom? How does one turn freedom into a system?

To find out cost plenty. I have a son of forty-two who hates me. We needn't go into that. The point is that the mob didn't come and open my cell door. The erratic mob was there, but as it happened, I had to open the door myself. Because I too was compliant and fundamentally thwarted, even if, while I was married, I was sneaking out of the house fucking whomever I could. That kind of sixties deliverance was what I'd had in mind from the beginning, but in the beginning, my beginning, there was nothing resembling a communal endorsement of anything like it, no social torrent to sweep you up and carry you along. There were only obstacles, one of which was one's civil nature, one of which was one's provincial beginnings, one of which was one's education in genteel notions of seriousness that one could not buck alone. The trajectory of my upbringing and my education was to delude me into entering a domestic vocation for which I had no tolerance. The family man, conscientious, married and with the kid—and then the revolution begins. The whole thing explodes and there are these girls all around me, and what was I to do, continue on married and having my adulteries and thinking, This is it, this is the bound way you live?

I didn't find my way because I was born in the forest and raised by wild beasts and therefore came by release naturally. I wasn't born smart about any of this. I too lacked the authority to do openly what I wanted to do. It's not the man you're sitting across from who got married in 1956. To gain a confident idea of the scope of one's autonomy you needed guidance that was nowhere to be found, not in my little world anyway, which is why marrying and having a child seemed, in '56, the natural thing even for me to do.

One wasn't an enfranchised man in the sexual realm while I was growing up. One was a second-story man. One was a thief in the sexual realm. You "copped" a feel. You stole sex. You cajoled, you begged, you flattered, you insisted—all sex had to be struggled for, against the values if not the will of the girl. The set of rules was that you had to impose your will on her. That's how she was taught to maintain the spectacle of her virtue. That an ordinary girl should volunteer, without endless importuning, to break the code and commit the sex act would have confused me. Because no one of either sex had any sense of an erotic birthright. Unknown. She might, if she fell for you, agree to a hand job—which meant essentially using your hand with hers as an insert—but that someone would consent to anything without the ritual of psychological besiegement, of un-remitting, monomaniacal tenacity and exhortation, well, that was unthinkable. There was no way to get a blow job, certainly, other than by dint of superhuman perseverance. I got one in four years of college. That's all you were allowed. In the Catskill hick town where my family ran a small resort hotel and I came of age in the forties, the only way to consensual sex was either with a prostitute or with someone who'd been your girl for the better part of your life and whom everybody figured you were going to marry. And there you paid your dues because often enough you did marry her.

My parents? They were parents. I was sentimentally educated, believe me. When my father, pushed by my mother, had at last to have the discussion with me about sex, I was already sixteen, it was 1946, and I was disgusted by his way of not knowing what to tell me, this gentle soul born in a Lower East Side tenement in 1898. Mainly what he wanted to tell me was what usually emanated from the kindly Jewish father of that generation: "You're a peach, you're a plum, you can ruin your life . . ." Of course, he didn't know that I already had a venereal disease from the loose girl in town whom everyone fucked. So much for parents in those far-off days.

Look, heterosexual men going into marriage are like priests going into the Church: they take the vow of chastity, only seemingly without knowing it until three, four, five years down the line. The nature of ordinary marriage is no less suffocating to the virile heterosexual—given the sexual preferences of a virile heterosexual—than it is to the gay or the lesbian.

Though now even gays want to get married. Church wedding. Two, three hundred witnesses. And wait till they see what becomes of the desire that got them into being gay in the first place. I expected more from those guys, but it turns out there's no realism in them either. Though I suppose it has to do with AIDS. The Fall and Rise of the Condom is the sexual story of the second half of the twentieth century. The condom came back. And with the condom, the return of all that got blown out in the sixties. What man can say he enjoys sex with a condom the way he does without? What's really in it for him? That's why the organs of digestion have, in our time, come to vie for supremacy as a sexual orifice. The crying need for the mucous membrane. To get rid of the condom, they have to have a steady partner, therefore they marry. The gays are militant: they want marriage and they want openly to join the army and be accepted. The two institutions I loathed. And for the same reason: regimentation.

The last person to take these matters seriously was John Milton, three hundred and fifty years ago. Ever read his tracts on divorce? In his day, made him many enemies. They're here, they're among my books, margins heavily annotated back in the sixties. "Did our Saviour open so to us this hazardous and accidental door of marriage to shut upon us like the gate of death . . . ?" No, men don't know any-thing—or willingly act as though they don't—about the tough, tragic side of what they're getting into. At best they stoically think, Yes, I understand that sooner or later I'm going to relinquish sex in this marriage, but it's in order to have other, more valu-able things. But do they understand what they're for-saking? To be chaste, to live without sex, well, how will you take the defeats, the compromises, the frus-trations? By making more money, by making all the money you can? By making all the children you can? That helps, but it's nothing like the other thing. Because the other thing is based in your physical being, in the flesh that is born and the flesh that dies. Because only when you fuck is everything that you dislike in life and everything by which you are de-feated in life purely, if momentarily, revenged. Only then are you most cleanly alive and most cleanly yourself. It's not the sex that's the corruption—it's the rest. Sex isn't just friction and shallow fun. Sex is also the revenge on death. Don't forget death. Don't ever forget it. Yes, sex too is limited in its power. I know very well how limited. But tell me, what power is greater?

Anyway, Carolyn Lyons, nearly two and a half dec-ades later and thirty-five pounds heavier. I'd loved her old size but I soon got to like the new size, with all that monumentality at the base sustaining her slender torso. I let it inspire me as though I were Gaston Lachaise. Her wide rump and heavy thighs spoke to me of all that was female in her baled. And her movement beneath me, the subtlety of her excitement, inspired another pastoral comparison: the plowing of a softly billowing field. Carolyn the undergraduate flower you pollinated, Carolyn at forty-five you farmed. The disparity in scale between the sinuous old upper half and the substantial new lower half replicated an intriguing tension in my overall perception of her. She was for me an exciting hybrid of the intelligent, tremulous, daring pioneer who couldn't stop raising her hand in class, the beautiful dissident in gypsy drag, Janie Wyatt's most sensible sidekick, who knew all the answers back in 1965, and the assertive business executive she had become in middle age, packing the potential to overpower you.

You might have expected that as time wore on and the hothouse passion of the teacher-student taboo ceased feeding into the permissible pleasures of the present moment, our meetings would run out of nostalgic appeal. But a year had passed and that hadn't happened. Because of the ease and the calm and the physical trust inherent in a resumption of play between teammates of old and because of Carolyn's realism—the sense of proportion adult indignities had predictably imposed on the romantic expectations of a highly credentialed upper-middle-class girl—I reaped rewards that it was impossible to draw from my crazy bingeing on Consuela's breasts. Our harmonious, no-nonsense evenings in bed—scheduled by cell phone, on the run, for whenever Carolyn touched down at Kennedy from one of her business trips—now provided the only point of contact with my pre-Consuela confidence. I never needed more the straightforward satiation Carolyn so dependably afforded now that she'd been tested as a woman and stoically survived. Each of us was getting exactly what we wanted. It was a joint venture, our sexual partnership, that profited us both and that was strongly colored by Carolyn's crisp executive manner. Here pleasure and equilibrium combined.

Then came the night that Consuela pulled out her tampon and stood there in my bathroom, with one knee dipping toward the other and, like Mantegna's Saint Sebastian, bleeding in a trickle down her thighs while I watched. Was it thrilling? Was I delighted? Was I mesmerized? Sure, but again I felt like a boy. I had set out to demand the most from her, and when she shamelessly obliged, I wound up again intimidating myself. There seemed nothing to be done—

if I wished not to be humbled completely by her exotic matter-of-factness—except to fall to my knees to lick her clean. Which she allowed to happen without comment. Making me into a still smaller boy. One's impossible character. The stupidity of being oneself. The unavoidable comedy of being anyone at all. Each new excess weakening me further—yet what is an insatiable man to do?

The expression on her face? I was at her feet. I was on the floor. My own face was pressed to her flesh like a feeding infant's, so I could see nothing of hers. But I told you, I don't believe she was intimidated. There was no overwhelming new emotion for Consuela to deal with. Once we'd got past the preliminaries as lovers, she seemed able to assimilate easily enough whatever her nudity provoked in me. It made no sense to her that a married man like George O'Hearn should be kissing a fully clothed young woman in a public place at eight in the morning—*that* was chaos to Consuela. But this? This was just a novel divertissement. This was coming to her, the physical fate she so lightly wore. Surely the attention being accorded by the cultural authority down on his knees wasn't something that made her feel unimportant. Consuela had been alluring to boys all her life, loved by her family all her life, adored by her father all her life, so that self-possession, repose, a kind of statuesque equanimity, was instinctively the form her theatricality took. Somehow Consuela had been spared the awkwardness that is given to just about everyone.

That was a Thursday night. Friday night Carolyn came right from the airport to me, and on Saturday morning I was at the table, already over breakfast, when she marched into the kitchen from the shower wearing my terrycloth robe and holding in her hand a bloody tampon half wrapped in toilet paper. First she showed it to me and then she threw it at me. "You are fucking other women. Tell me the truth," Carolyn said, "and then I'm going. I don't like this. I had two husbands who fucked other women. I didn't like it then and I don't like it now. And least of all with you. You make the kind of connection we have —and then you do this. You have everything you want as you want it—fucking like ours outside of domesticity and outside of romance—and then you do this. There aren't many like me, David. I have an interest in what you have an interest in. I understand what's what. Harmonious hedonism. I am one in a million, idiot—so how could you possibly do this?" She spoke not angrily like a wife fortified by the ironclad historical claim but like a courtesan of renown, out of indisputable erotic superiority. She had a right to do so: most people bring to bed with them the worst of their biography—Carolyn brought only the best. No, she wasn't angry; she was humiliated and undone. Once more, her bountiful sexuality had been deemed less than enough by another unworthy, unsatisfiable man. She said, "I'm not going to quarrel with you. I want to know the truth and then you'll never see me again."

I tried to be as composed as possible, only mildly curious, when I asked, "Where did you find this?" The tampon was now on the kitchen table, lying between the butter dish and the teapot. "In the bathroom. In the trash basket." "Well, I don't know whose it is or how it got there." "Why don't you put it on your bagel and eat it?" Carolyn suggested. All I said, by way of reply, was "I would, gladly, if that would make you happy. But I don't know whose it is. I think I should know whose it is before I eat it." "I can't put up with this, David. It makes me furious." "I have a thought. I have a suggestion. My friend George," I said, "has a key to the apartment. He's won a Pulitzer, he gives readings, he teaches at the New School, he meets women, girls, he sleeps with everyone he meets, and since obviously he cannot bring them home to his wife and four children, and since to find a hotel room in New York is sometimes impossible, and since he is always short on funds anyway, and since the women are married, many of them, and he can't take them to *their* houses"—every word I spoke, true so far—"he sometimes brings them here."

Now that was not true. That was the same durable lie with which I had saved myself before when, over the years, some woman's incriminating personal belonging—though admittedly never one quite so primordial—was discovered that had been either negligently or deliberately left behind. The durable lie of the run-of-the-mill roué. Nothing to boast about there.

"So," Carolyn said, "George fucks all these women in your bed." "Not all of them. But some, yes. He uses the bed in the guest room. He is my friend. His marriage is not paradise. He reminds me of myself when I was married. George feels pure only in his transgressions. His obedient side makes him sick. How can I say no?" "You're too meticulous for that, David. You're too orderly for that. I don't believe a word you're saying. Everything in your life is just so, everything is considered, everything is deliberate—" "Well, that alone should convince you—" "Someone was here, David." "No one," I said, "not

with me. I really don't know whose tampon it is."
It was a fierce, tense situation, but by bluntly lying
right into her face, I survived and, fortunately, she
did not leave me when I needed her most. She left
only later, and at my request.

Excuse me, I have to take that call. I must answer.
Excuse . . .

Sorry to be away so long. It wasn't even the call
I'm waiting for. Sorry to leave you alone like this, but
it was my son. He phoned to tell me how insulted he
still is by everything I said at our last meeting and to
be sure I got the angry letter he wrote.

Look, I never thought that it would be easy for us,
and for all I know he might have started hating me
even without encouragement. I knew it was a difficult escape, and I knew I could take only myself over
the wall. If I'd taken him, had that even been possible, it wouldn't have made sense because he was eight
years old and I couldn't have lived the way I wanted
to. I had to betray him, and for that I am not for-
given and never will be.

This past year he became an adulterer at the age
of forty-two; ever since he's begun showing up unan-
nounced at my door. Eleven, twelve o'clock at night,
one, even two in the morning, and there he is on

the intercom. "It's me. Let me up, ring me in!" He argues with his wife, storms out of the house, gets in the car, and, despite himself, he winds up here. After he'd grown up, we hardly saw each other for years on end; for months we didn't so much as speak on the phone. You can imagine my surprise at his first midnight visit. What are you here for, I ask him. He's in trouble. He's in a crisis. He's suffering. Why? He has a girlfriend. A young woman of twenty-six who recently came to work for him. He runs a little company that restores damaged works of art. That was his mother's occupation until she retired: art conservator. He went into her field after getting his Ph.D. from NYU, joined forces with her, and now the business is quite successful, with eighteen people working for him in a SoHo loft. A lot of gallery work, private collectors, auction houses, consultant to Sotheby's, and so on. Kenny's a big, good-looking man, dresses impeccably, speaks authoritatively, writes intelligently, converses easily in French and German—out in the art world he's obviously impressive. But not with me. My deficiencies are at the root of his suffering. Put him anywhere near me and the wound within begins to hemorrhage. At his work he's active, healthy, solid, not insufficient in any way, but I have only to speak and I paralyze everything strong in him. And I have merely to remain silent while *he* speaks in order to undermine everything that makes him effectual. I'm the father he can't defeat, the father in whose presence his powers are overwhelmed. Why? Perhaps because I wasn't present. I was absent and terrifying. I was absent and entirely too full of meaning. I failed him. That's sufficient reason to make a calm relationship out of the question. There's nothing in our history to impede the filial instinct to lay every impediment at the father's feet.

I am Kenny's Karamazov father, the base, the monstrous force with whom he, a saint of love, a man who must behave well all the time, feels himself wronged and parricidal, as though he were all the brothers Karamazov in one. Parents play a legendary role in the minds of their children, and that my ordained legend has been Dostoyevskian I know from as far back as the late seventies, when I received in the mail a copy of a paper Kenny had written as a Princeton sophomore, an A paper on *The Brothers Karamazov*. It wasn't hard to ascertain the book's relevance as an exaggerated fantasy of his own condition. Kenny was one of those overheated kids for whom whatever he read had a personal significance that eradicated everything else germane to literature.

He was by then wholly preoccupied with our estrangement and, inevitably, the focus of his paper was the father. A depraved sensualist. A solitary old lecher. An old man with his young girls. A great buffoon who sets up a harem of loose women in his house. A father who, you may remember, abandons his first child, ignores all his children, "for a child," Dostoyevsky writes, "would have gotten in the way of his debaucheries." You've not read *The Brothers Karamazov*? But you must, if only for the amusing portrait of the profligate wickedness of the shameful father.

Whenever Kenny would come to me distraught back in his adolescence, it was always over the same issue. It still is: something has threatened his idea of himself as a punctiliously upright person. One way or another, I would encourage him to modulate that idea, to temper it a bit, but suggesting that would make him furious and he would turn around and run back to his mother. I remember I asked him once, when he was thirteen and starting high school and beginning to look and sound like something more than a child, whether he would like to stay with me for the summer in a house I'd rented up in the Catskills, not far from my parents' hotel. It was an afternoon in May and we were at a Mets game.

Another of our painful Sundays together. He was so chagrined by the invitation that he had to rush off to vomit in the men's room at Shea. In the old days, in the Old World, fathers used to initiate their sons into sex by taking them to the whorehouse, and it was as though that was what I had proposed. He vomited because if he came to be with me, one of my girls might be around. Maybe two. Maybe more. Because in his mind my house *was* the whorehouse. Yet his vomiting bespoke not just revulsion with me but, even more, revulsion with his revulsion. Why? Because of what he desperately wanted, because even with a father with whom he's angry and disappointed, the moment together with him is so powerful and the yearning for him is so great. He was still a boy in a helpless predicament. This was before he cauterized the wound by turning himself into a prig.

In his last year of college he thought, correctly, that he might have impregnated one of his classmates. He was too alarmed at first to tell his mother, so he came to me. I assured him that if the girl actually turned out to be pregnant, he hadn't to marry her. This wasn't 1901. If she was determined to have the baby, as she was already insisting, then that was her choice, not his. Pro-choice I was, but that didn't mean pro her choice for him. I urged him to remind her as often as he could that, at the age of twenty-one and just graduating from college, he didn't want a child, couldn't support a child, didn't intend in any way to be responsible for a child. If, at twenty-one, she wanted the responsibility all on her own, that was a decision made by her for herself alone. I offered him money to pay for an abortion. I told him I was behind him and not to cave in. "But what if she won't change her mind? What," he asked me, "if she flatly refuses?" I said that if she didn't come to her senses, she would have to live with the consequences. I reminded him that nobody could make him do what he didn't want to do. I said what I wished some forceful man had said to me when I was on the brink of making *my* mistake. I said, "Living in a country like ours, whose key documents are all about emancipation, all directed at guaranteeing individual liberty, living in a free system that is basically indifferent to how you behave as long as the behavior is lawful, the misery that comes your way is most likely to be self-generated. It would be another matter if you were living in Nazi-occupied Europe or in Communist-dominated Europe or in Mao Zedong's China. There they manufacture the misery for you; you don't have to take a single wrong step in order never to want to get up in the morning. But here, free of totalitarianism, a man like you has to provide himself his own misery. You, moreover, are intelligent, articulate, good-looking, well educated—you are *made* to thrive in a country like this one. Here the only tyrant lying in wait will be convention, which is not to be taken lightly either. Read Tocqueville, if you haven't yet. He's not outdated, not on the subject of 'men being forced through the same sieve.' The point is that you shouldn't think that you miraculously have to become a beatnik or a bohemian or a hippie to elude the trammels of convention. Successfully doing so doesn't require exaggerations of conduct or oddities of dress that are alien to your temperament and your upbringing. Not at all. All you have to do, Ken, is to find your force. You have it, I know you have it—it is immobilized only by the newness of the predicament. If you want to live intelligently beyond the blackmail of the slogans and the unexamined rules, you have only to find your own . . ." Et cetera, et cetera. The Declaration of Independence. The Bill of Rights. The Gettysburg Address. The Emancipation Proclamation. The Fourteenth Amendment. All three of the Civil War amendments. I went over everything with him. I found the Tocqueville for him. I figured, he's twenty-one, at long last we can talk. I out-Poloniused Polonius. What I was telling him, after all, wasn't so far out, certainly not for 1979. Nor would it have been back when I needed it drummed into *my* head. Conceived in liberty—that's just good American common sense. But when I was finished, what did he do? He began to recount to me all her outstanding qualities. I asked, "What about *your* qualities?" But he didn't seem to hear me, just started in again to tell me how smart she was, how pretty she was, what a funny girl she was, he told me about her terrific family, and a couple months later he married her.

I know all the objections that a pure and moral young man can give to claiming personal sovereignty. I know all the admirable labels to attach to not asserting one's sovereignty. Well, Kenny's difficulty is that he must be admirable whatever the cost. He lives in fear of a woman telling him he's not. "Selfish" is the word that cripples him. You selfish bastard. He's terrified of that judgment, so that's the judgment that rules. Yes, count on Kenny for the admirable thing, whatever it may be, which is why when Todd, his oldest child, entered high school and my daughter-in-law said that they had to have more children, he became a father three more times in the next six years. At just the point when he was sick and tired of her. Because he's so admirable, he cannot leave his wife for the girlfriend, he cannot leave the girlfriend for the wife, and of course he cannot leave his young children. God knows he cannot leave his mother. The one he can leave is me. But he grew up with the list of grievances, and so, in the years immediately after the divorce, whenever I saw him I had to plead my case, at the zoo, at the movies, at the ballgame, demonstrating that I'm not what his mother says I am.

I gave it up because I *am* what she says I am. He was her creature, and by the time he went off to college, I wasn't going to contend any longer for somebody I made sick to his stomach. I gave it up because I didn't care to feign the feminine need against which Kenny has no defense. To the pathos of feminine need my son is most cruelly addicted. During those years he was alone with his mother cultivating this archaic addiction—which, by the way, in the days of the dependent woman enslaved all the best men—he and I would always spend two weeks together in the summer at my parents' little hotel. A relief for me because my parents took over. They were starved for all the family doings, and because of our history he and I couldn't begin to make a go of it. But once the grandparents were gone, once he was in graduate school, married, a father . . . Yet he always called me when one of his children was born.

Kind of him, given his feelings about me. That I lost I of course knew long ago. But Kenny lost too. The consequences of my being what I am are long term. These domestic disasters are dynastic.

Though suddenly, once a month, once every six weeks, he comes to drain himself in my presence of what's poisoning him. There's fear in his eyes, there's rage in his heart, there's weariness in his voice; even his elegant clothes no longer fit. The wife is unhappy and angry about the girlfriend, the girlfriend is complaining and resentful of the wife, and the children are frightened and cry out in their sleep. As for conjugal sex, a heinous duty he stoically performs, that is beyond even his fortitude now. Arguments abound, irritable bowel syndrome abounds, placation abounds, threats abound, as do counterthreats. But when I ask, "Then why not leave?" he tells me that leaving would destroy his family. No one would survive, everybody would have a breakdown, the suffering would be too great all around. Instead, everyone must cling to everyone else.

What's implicit is how much more honorable he is than the father who walked out on him when he was eight. His life has a significance that mine does not. This is his strong suit. This is where he dominates and is superior to me.

"Kenny," I tell him, "why not finally confront

your father as a reality? Confront at long last your father's prick. This is the reality of a father. We lie to a child about these things. There cannot be candor about the father's prick to a child. That many fathers cannot contain themselves in a marriage—it's just as well that's a secret from the little ones. But you are a man. You know the score. You know all these artists. You know all these dealers. You must have some idea of how adults live their lives. Is this still the biggest scandal imaginable?"

All he and I do is berate each other, though not in the established tradition. Beyond the pages of Dostoyevsky, the story is traditionally the opposite: the father's the customary constraining authority, the son is incorrigible, and the castigation flows the other way. Yet he continues to come here, and whenever he rings the bell, I let him up. "Your girlfriend is how old?" I ask. "And having an affair with a married man of forty-two, a father of four, who is her boss? So she is not such a paragon either. Only you are the paragon. You and your mother." You should hear him about this girl. A chemist who also has a degree in art history. *And* plays the oboe. Wonderful, I tell him. Even in your adultery you are better than I am. He won't even call it adultery. His adultery is different from everyone else's. It's too committed an arrangement to be called adultery. And commitment is what I lack. My adulteries weren't serious enough to suit him.

Well, that is true. I tried not to have it be serious. But for him adultery is the recruitment of the new wife. He went to meet her family. That's what he was just telling me, how he flew down with her yesterday to meet them. "You flew to Florida," I asked him, "back and forth in a day to meet her parents? But this is adultery. What do her parents have to do with it?" He tells me that at the outset, at the airport, her parents are cold and very skeptical, but by the time they all sit down together in the condo for dinner, they tell her that they love him. Love him like their own son. Everybody loves everybody. It was worth the trip. "And did you meet your girlfriend's sister and her lovely children?" I asked him. "Did you meet her brother and *his* lovely children?" Oh boy, the little prison that is his current marriage he is about to trade in for a maximum-security facility. Headed once again straight for the slammer. I tell him, "Kenny, you want license and approval both? Well, it so happens that I willingly give license and approval both." But he doesn't stop at that. It's not enough that he's got the one father in this whole big country who will endorse what he's doing and maybe even set him up with another piece of ass with a wonderful family in Florida. I must also yield to the superiority. "The oboe too," I said. "Isn't that just grand? I'm sure she writes poetry in her spare time. I'm sure her parents do too." Credentials, credentials, credentials. This one cannot fuck if he doesn't have a dominatrix over him snapping a whip. This one cannot fuck if the girl is not dressed like a chambermaid. Some can fuck only midgets, some only criminals, some only chickens. My son can fuck only a girl with the right moral credentials. Please, I tell him, it's a perversity, no better or worse than any other. Recognize it for what it is and don't feel so special.

Here. The letter he was afraid might have been lost in the mail. Dated later the very night last week that he came to see me. As though over this past year of our trading insults I haven't got ten others like it. "You're a hundred times worse than I thought." That's the beginning. That's the boilerplate. Then this. Let me read it to you. "You keep going on. I couldn't believe it. The things you said to me. You must assert yourself all the time, prove that your choice in life was the right one and mine the cowardly one, the grotesque one, the wrong one. I came to you distressed in the extreme, and the mental violence you directed at me. The sixties—he owes all that he is today to how seriously he took Janis Joplin.

Without Janis Joplin never could he have emerged at the age of seventy as the very picture of a pathetic old fool. The long white pageboy of important hair, the turkey wattle half hidden behind the fancy foulard—when will you begin to rouge your cheeks, Herr von Aschenbach? What do you think you look like? Do you have any idea? All that devotion to the Higher Life. Manning the aesthetic barricades on Channel Thirteen. The singlehanded battle to maintain cultural standards in a mass society. But what about observing ordinary standards of decency? Of course you didn't have the guts to stay in academic life and be serious; you've never been serious for a day in your life. Janie Wyatt, where is *she* now? How many failed marriages? How many breakdowns? In what psychiatric hospital has she been a patient for lo these many years? These girls go to college, and they shouldn't be protected from you? You are the living argument *for* protecting them. I have two daughters, your granddaughters, and if I thought that my daughters were to go to a college and have as their teacher a man like my father . . ."

And on like that . . . until . . . let's see . . . yes, he's stronger here. "My kids are frightened and screaming because their parents are having an argument and Daddy is so angry he is leaving the house. Do you know what it's like for me with my children when I come home at night? Do you know what it's like to hear your children cry? How *could* you know? And I protected you. *I* protected *you.* I tried not to believe that Mother was right. I came to your defense, I stuck up for you. I had to, you were my father. In my mind, I tried to excuse you, I tried to understand you. But the *sixties?* That explosion of childishness, that vulgar, mindless, collective regression, and that explains everything and excuses it all? Can't you come up with any better alibi? Seducing defenseless students, pursuing one's sexual interests at the expense of everyone else—that's so very necessary, is it? No, necessity is staying in a difficult marriage and raising a little child and meeting the responsibilities of an adult. All those years I thought Mother was exaggerating. But it wasn't exaggeration. I little knew until tonight what it was that she lived through. The pain you caused her, and for what? The burden you put on her—the burden you put on *me*, on a child, to be everything in the world to his mother, and for what? So you could be 'free'? I cannot bear you. I never could."

And next month he'll be back again to tell me how he can't bear me. And the month after that. And the month after that. I didn't lose him after all. His father is finally a resource. "It's me. Let me up. Ring me in!" His situation brings him no self-irony, but I believe he gets more than he lets on. He doesn't get anything? He must. He is by no means stupid. He can't be besieged forever by his childhood drama. He is? Well, perhaps so. You're probably right. He will be raw about this for the rest of his life. One of the innumerable jokes: a man of forty-two, adjoined to the thirteen-year-old boy's existence and tormented by it still. Perhaps it's just as it was at the ballgame. He's dying to break out. He's dying to get away from his mother, he's dying to go off with his father, and all he can do is vomit his heart out.

My affair with Consuela lasted for a little more than a year and a half. Only occasionally did we ever again go out for dinner or to the theater. She was too afraid of the prying press and of winding up on Page Six, and that was fine with me, because whenever I saw her I always wanted to fuck her right away and not have first to sit through some shitty play. "You know how the media are, you know what they do to people, and if I go there with you . . ." "Fine, don't worry," I would say agreeably, "we'll just stay home." Eventually she would stay overnight, and we would have breakfast together. We saw each other once or twice a week, and, even after the incident with the tampon, Carolyn failed to discover Consuela's existence. Still, I was never at peace about Consuela; never could I forget about the five boys she had fucked before me, two of whom turned out to be brothers, one her lover at eighteen, the other when she was twenty—Cuban brothers, Bergen County's wealthy Villareal brothers, and another cause for suffering. If it weren't for the calming influence of Carolyn and our wonderful nights together, I don't know what would have happened to me.

The agitation of having Consuela—as opposed to the agitation of not having Consuela—ended only when she received her master's degree and had a party over in New Jersey at her parents' house. Of course it was as well for both of us that it ended, but it wasn't my plan to end it, and I was bereft afterward. I was depressed off and on for nearly three years. Tormented all the while I was with her, a hundred times more tormented for having lost her. It was a bad time and it wouldn't stop. George O'Hearn was an ace. He talked me through many an evening when I found myself getting too low. And I had my piano, which was what pulled me through.

I told you that over the years I bought a lot of music, the piano literature, and so I played all the time, whenever I finished my other work. I played all thirty-two Beethoven sonatas during those years, every note of them to drive Consuela out of my thoughts. Nobody should be forced to hear a tape of that playing, which doesn't exist anyway. Some passages were in tempo, but most weren't, yet on I played regardless. Freakish, but it's what I did. With keyboard music you have the feeling of reproducing what the composers were doing, and so you're in their minds to some degree. Not in the most mysterious part, where the music originates, but still, you're not merely passively absorbing an aesthetic experience. You are, in your own clumsy way, somehow producing it yourself, and this is how I tried escaping the loss of Consuela. I played the Mozart sonatas. I played Bach's piano music. I played it, I'm familiar with it, which is a different thing from playing it well. I played Elizabethan pieces by Byrd and people like that. I played Purcell. I played Scarlatti. I have all the Scarlatti sonatas, all five hundred and fifty of them. I won't say I played all of them, but I played a lot of them. Haydn's piano music. I know it cold now. Schumann. Schubert. And this, as I told you, is on the basis of very little training. But it was an awful time, a futile time, and it was either study Beethoven and enter his mind or stay in my own mind and replay all the scenes of her I could remember—replay, worst of all, the reckless thing I did by not going to her graduation party.

But, you see, I could never figure how ordinary she was. This girl who takes her tampon out for me, and then because I don't show up at her graduation party, she's finished with me? The casualness of something so powerful ending as it did is unbelievable to me. The abruptness with which it ends, I replay *that*, thinking that the secret of the abruptness is that Consuela didn't want it to go on. Why? Because she didn't desire me, never desired me, because she experimented with me, really, to see how overwhelming her breasts could be. But she herself was never getting what she wanted. She was getting that from the Villareal brothers. Of course. There they all were at the party, pressing in on her, surrounding her, dark, handsome, muscular, mannerly, young, and she realized, What am I doing with this old man? So I was right all along—and therefore it was right for it to end. She went as far as she wanted to go. All I could have done by forging ahead was to arrange more torture for myself. The smartest thing I did was not to show up there. Because I had been yielding and yielding in ways that I didn't understand. The longing never disappeared even while I had her. The primary emotion, as I've said, was longing. It's still longing. There's no relief from the longing and my sense of myself as a supplicant. There it is: you have it when you're with her and you have it when you're without her. So who ended it? Did I end it by not going to the party, or did she end it by seizing upon my not going to the party? This is the endless debate I had and why, to stop my mind from revolving around the loss of Consuela—to stop myself from falsely particularizing this one event, the party, as the clue to everything I'd mismanaged—I often had to get up in the middle of the night and play the piano until dawn.

All that had happened was that she invited me to Jersey to celebrate her getting her degree and I had to say yes, but as I was driving across the bridge, I thought, Her parents will be there, her grandparents, the Cuban relatives, all the old childhood friends will be there, those brothers will be there, and I will be introduced as the teacher who is on television. And it was just too silly after a year and a half for me to pretend I was nothing to this young woman but a kindly mentor, especially in the presence of those fucking Villareals. I was too old for this nonsense, so I stopped on the Jersey side of the bridge and phoned her and told her my car had broken down and I couldn't come. A transparent lie—I had a Porsche not two years old—and so that very night, from New Jersey, she faxed me a letter on the family fax machine, not the most explosive letter I have ever received from anyone, but nonetheless, I could never have imagined Consuela uncontrollable like this.

But I could never imagine Consuela altogether. What more didn't I know about her because of being blinded by my obsession? Shouting at me in the letter: "You're always playing the wise old man who knows everything." Shouting: "I saw you just this morning on television, playing the role of the one who always knows better, knowing what is good culture and what is bad culture, knowing what people should read and what they shouldn't read, knowing all about music and all about art, and then, to celebrate this important moment in my life, I have a party, I want to have a wonderful party, I want to have you around, you who mean everything to me, and you're not there." And I had already sent her a present, sent flowers, but she was so furious, so angry . . . "Mr. Arrogant Intellectual Critic, the great authority on everything, teaching everybody what to think and setting everyone right! *Me da asco!*"

That's how she ended it. Never before, not even

affectionately, had Consuela availed herself of Spanish with me. *Me da asco.* Ordinary idiom meaning, "It makes me sick."

This is all six and a half years ago. The strange thing was that three months later I got a postcard from her, from some Third World country with a first-class resort—Belize, Honduras, some such place —and it was completely friendly. Then six months later she phoned me. She was applying for a job in advertising, the kind of job, she said, I would hate her for, but would I write a letter of recommendation anyway? As her former professor. Which I wrote. Then I got a postcard (a Modigliani nude from the Modern) saying she got the job and that she was very happy. And then nothing more from her. One night I found her name in a new Manhattan phone book, the address of an apartment her father must have bought for her on the Upper East Side. But going back was a bad idea and I didn't try.

George, for one, wouldn't let me. George O'Hearn, though fifteen years my junior, was my worldly confessor. He was the friend closest to me during the year and a half I was with Consuela, and only afterward did he tell me how concerned he'd been, how he'd kept a careful watch over me as I denuded myself of my realism, my pragmatism, my cynicism and thought of nothing but losing her. He's the one who wouldn't let me answer her postcard, which I was dying to do, which I believed I was being invited to do by the cylindrical stalk of a waist, the wide pelvic span, and the gently curving thighs, by the patch of flame that is the hair that marks the spot where she is forked—by the trademark Modigliani nude, the accessible, elongated dream girl he ritualistically painted and that Consuela had chosen to send, so immodestly, through the U.S. mail. A nude whose breasts, full and canting a bit to the side, might well have been modeled on her own. A nude represented with her eyes closed, defended, like Consuela, by nothing other than her erotic power, at once, like Consuela, elemental and elegant. A golden-skinned nude inexplicably asleep over a velvety black abyss that, in my mood, I associated with the grave. One long, undulating line, she lies there awaiting you, still as death.

George hadn't even wanted me to write the recommendation for the job. He said, "You'll always be powerless with this girl. You'll never be in charge. There's something there," George told me, "that makes you crazy and always will. If you don't cut the connection for good, in the end that something will destroy you. You're no longer merely answering a natural need with her. This is the pathology in its purest form. Look," he told me, "see it as a critic, see it from a professional point of view. You violated the law of aesthetic distance. You sentimentalized the aesthetic experience with this girl—you personalized it, you sentimentalized it, and you lost the sense of separation essential to your enjoyment. Do you know when that happened? The night she took the tampon out. The necessary aesthetic separation collapsed not while you watched her bleeding—that was all right, that was fine—but when you couldn't restrain yourself and went down on your knees. And what the hell compelled you? What lies behind the comedy of this Cuban girl taking a guy like you, the professor of desire, to the mat? Drinking her blood? I'd say that constituted the abandonment of an independent critical position, Dave. Worship me, she says, worship the mystery of the bleeding goddess, and you do it. You stop at nothing. You lick it. You consume it. You digest it. *She* penetrates *you*. What next, David? A glass of her urine? How long before you would have begged her for feces? I'm not against it because it's unhygienic. I'm not against it because it's disgusting. I'm against it because it's falling in love. The only obsession everyone wants: 'love.' People think that in falling in love they make themselves whole? The Platonic union of souls? I think otherwise. I think you're whole before you begin. And the love fractures you. You're whole, and then you're cracked open. She was a foreign body introduced into your wholeness. And for a year and a half you struggled to incorporate it. But you'll never be whole until you expel it. You either get rid of it or incorporate it through self-distortion. And that's what you did and what drove you mad."

Hard to sanction those words, and not only because of George's mythopoeticizing turn of mind; just hard to believe in the disastrous potential of a character so seemingly unintimidating as family-bound, protected, suburban Consuela. George wouldn't let up. "Attachment is ruinous and your enemy. Joseph Conrad: He who forms a tie is lost. That you should sit there looking like you do is absurd. You tasted it. Isn't that enough? Of what do you ever get more than a taste? That's all we're given in life, that's all we're given *of* life. A taste. There is no more."

George was right, of course, and only repeating to me what I know. He who forms a tie *is* lost, attachment *is* my enemy, so I employed what Casanova called "the schoolboy's remedy"—I masturbated instead. I would imagine myself sitting at my piano while she stood naked beside me. We had once enacted just such a tableau in the flesh, so I was as much remembering as imagining. I had asked her if she would take off her clothes and let me look at her while I played the Mozart Sonata in C Minor, and she obliged. I don't know that I played it any better than I ordinarily did, but that was never the point. In another recurring fantasy, I am telling her, "This is a metronome. The little light flashes and it makes a periodic noise. That's all it does. You adjust the pace to what you want. Not only amateurs like me but professionals, even great concert pianists, have the problem of what's called rushing." Once again, I envision her standing by the piano with her clothes at her feet, as on the night when, fully dressed, I played the C Minor Sonata, serenading her nudity with the slow movement. (Sometimes she would come to me in a dream identified, like a spy, only as "K. 457.") "This is a quartz metronome," I say. "It's not the triangular-shaped thing you may have seen, with a pendulum, where the pendulum has a little weight on it, and the numbers are there. The numbers are the same as on a pendulum," and when she advances to examine the dial, her breasts pitch forward to cover my mouth and to stifle, momentarily, the pedagogy —the pedagogy that with Consuela is my greatest power. My only power.

"They're standard numbers," I tell her. "If you turn this to sixty, the beats will be seconds. Yes, like a heartbeat. Let me feel the tap of your heartbeat through the tip of my tongue." This she allows to happen, as she lets everything between us happen —without comment, almost without complicity. I tell her, "Actually, before it was invented about 1812 —the old one, that is—there are no metronome markings on music. What they did in the general treatises about tempo was to suggest that you employ the beat of the pulse as a certain kind of allegro. They'd say, 'Take your pulse and think of the tempo as that.' Let me take your pulse with the head of my prick. Sit on my prick, Consuela, and we'll play with time. Ah, it's not a fast allegro, is it? Not at all. Now, there's no Mozart piece with metronome markings, and why, why is that so? You remember when Mozart died . . ." But here I have my orgasm, the fantasy lesson is ended, and, for the moment, I am sick no longer with desire. Isn't that Yeats? "Consume my heart away; sick with desire / And fastened to a dying animal / It knows not what it is." Yeats. Yes. "Caught in that sensual music," and so on.

I played Beethoven and I masturbated. I played Mozart and I masturbated. I played Haydn, Schumann, Schubert, and masturbated with her image in mind. Because I could not forget the breasts, the ripe breasts, the nipples, and the way she could drape her breasts over my cock and fondle me like that. Another detail. A last detail and I'll stop. I am becoming a bit technical, but this is important. This was the touch that made Consuela a masterpiece of *volupté*. She's one of the few women I've known who come by pushing out the vulva, by involuntarily pushing it out like a bivalve's soft, unsegmented, bubbling-forth body. It took me by surprise the first time. You feel it and you get a sense of this other-world fauna, something from the sea. As though it were related to the oyster or the octopus or the squid, a creature from miles down and eons back. Normally you see the vagina and you can open it with your hands, but in her case it bloomed open, the cunt on its own emerging from its hiding place. The inner lips get extruded outward, swell outward, and it's very arousing, that slimy, silky swollenness, stimulating to touch and stimulating to see. The secret ecstatically exposed. Schiele would have given his eyeteeth to paint it. Picasso would have turned it into a guitar.

You can almost come by watching her come. She would turn her eyes away when it was like that for her. Her eyes turned up and you saw only the whites, and that was something to watch as well. All of her was something to watch. Whatever the agitation from the jealousy, whatever the humiliation and the endless uncertainty, I was always proud of making her come. Sometimes you don't even worry if a woman comes or not: it just happens, the woman seems to take care of it on her own and it's not your responsibility. It's not an issue with other women; the situation is enough, there's enough excitement and it's never in question. But with Consuela, yes, it was definitely a responsibility that was mine, and always, always it was a matter of pride.

I have a ridiculous forty-two-year-old son—ridiculous because he *is* my son, imprisoned in his marriage because of my escape from mine and the significance that's had for him and the protest against my personal life he's obstinately made of his own. Ridiculousness is the price he pays for having been molded too early into a Telemachus, heroic little defender of the untended mother. Yet, during my three years of off-and-on depression, I was a thousand times more ridiculous than Kenny. What do I mean by ridiculous? What is ridiculousness? Relinquishing one's freedom voluntarily—that is the definition of ridiculousness. If your freedom is taken from you by force, needless to say you're not ridiculous, except to the one who has forcibly taken it. But whoever gives his freedom away, whoever is dying to give it away, enters the realm of the ridiculous that brings the most famous of Ionesco's plays to mind and is a source of comedy throughout literature. The one who is free may be mad, stupid, repellent, in misery just because he is free, but he is not ridiculous. He has dimension as a being. I was myself ridiculous enough *with* Consuela. But during the years I was captive to the monotonous melodrama of the loss of her? My son, shaped by his contempt for my example, determined to be responsible where I was derelict, unable to free himself from anyone, beginning with me—my son may not wish to know any better, but I go about the world insisting that I do, and still the extraneous creeps in. Jealousy creeps in. Attachment creeps in. The eternal problem of attachment. No, not even fucking can stay totally pure and protected. And this is where I fail. The great propagandist for fucking and I can't do any better than Kenny. Of course there is no purity of the kind Kenny dreams of, but there is also no purity of the kind I dream of. When two dogs fuck there appears to be purity. *There*, we think, is pure fucking, among the beasts. But should we discuss it with them, we would probably find that even among dogs there are, in canine form, these crazy distortions of longing, doting, possessiveness, even of love.

This need. This derangement. Will it never stop? I don't even know after a while what I'm desperate for. Her tits? Her soul? Her youth? Her simple mind? Maybe it's worse than that—maybe now that I'm nearing death, I also long secretly not to be free.

Time passes. Time passes. I have new girlfriends. I have student girlfriends. Old girlfriends turn up from as long as twenty and thirty years back. Some are already divorced numerous times and some have been so busy establishing themselves professionally that they've not even had an opportunity to marry. The ones still on their own call me to complain about their dates. Dating is hateful, relationships are impossible, sex is a hazard. The men are narcissistic, humorless, crazy, obsessional, overbearing, crude, or they are great-looking, virile, and ruthlessly unfaithful, or they are emasculated, or they are impotent, or they are just too dumb. The twenty-odd-year-olds don't have these problems because they still have university-based friendships, and school, of course, is the great mixer, but the somewhat older women are, by their mid-thirties, so busy with their work that many of them, I discover, now resort to professional matchmakers to find men for them. And at a certain age they stop meeting new people anyway. As one of the disillusioned told me, "Who are the new people when you *do* meet them? They're the same old people in masks. There's nothing new about them at all. They're *people*."

The matchmakers range in price for what is a year's membership, during which time a certain number of introductions are guaranteed. Some matchmakers charge a couple hundred dollars, some a couple of thousand, and one I was told about, who specializes in what she calls "quality people," arranges introductions—up to twenty-five over two years—for no less than twenty-one thousand dollars. I thought I misheard when I was told this, but, yes, twenty-one thousand bucks is the fee. Well, it's hard on women engaging in this kind of transaction in order to find a man to marry them and to father children; no wonder they turn up late at night to sit and talk to their elderly ex-teacher, and sometimes, in their loneliness, even to stay over. Recently one of them was here trying to recover from having just been dumped in mid-meal on a first date by a man she described as "an extreme-vacation type, a super-duper adventurer into hunting lions and wild surfing." "It's rough out there, David," she told me.

"Because it isn't even dating, it's just *trying* to date. I've stoically accepted the matchmaking," she said, "but not even *that* works."

Elena, kindhearted Elena Hrabovsky, who's gone prematurely gray, maybe *from* the matchmaking. I said to her, "It must be a huge strain, the strangers, the silences, even the conversation," and she asked me, "Do you think it's supposed to be like this when you're as successful as I am?" Elena is an ophthalmologist, you see, up from the bottom of the working class by dint of immense fortitude. "Life baffles you," she told me, "and you become a very self-protective person and just say the hell with it. It's a great shame, but you run out of steam. Some of these men are more attractive than the average Joe. Educated. Most of them are making good livings. And I'm just never attracted to these people," she told me. "Why is it so boring to be with them? Maybe it's boring because I'm boring," she said. "Guys pick you up in nice cars. BMWs. Classical music on the way. Take you to nice little restaurants, and most of the time I sit there thinking, Please, Lord, just let me go home. I want kids, I want a family, I want a home," Elena said, "but though I have the emotional and physical wherewithal to spend six, seven, eight hours on my feet in the operating room, I don't have it anymore for this humiliation. *Some* of them find me impressive, at least." "Why shouldn't they? You're a retina specialist. You're an eye surgeon. You keep people from going blind." "I know. I mean flat-out rejection," she said, "I'm not built for that." "No one is," I told her, but that didn't seem to help. "I've given it a fair shot," she said, getting teary, "haven't I, David? Nineteen dates?" "My God," I said, "you more than have."

Elena was a mess that night. She stayed right through till dawn, when she rushed off to scrub up at the hospital. Neither of us got much sleep because I was lecturing on the necessity of her giving up on the idea of becoming coupled and because she was listening like the diligent, serious, note-taking student she'd been when we'd first met in my classroom. But whether I helped her I don't know. Elena's intelligent, tremendously capable, yet for her the desire for a child is the standard unthinking. Yes, the idea activates the propagative instinct, and that's the pathos of it, all right. But it's still part of the standard unthinking: you go on to the next step. It's so primitive for someone so accomplished. But this is the way she imagined adulthood long, long ago, before adulthood, before diseases of the retina became her life's passion.

What did I say to her? Why do you ask? You too need the lecture on the childishness of coupling? Of course it's childish. Family life is, today more than ever, when the ethos is created substantially by the children. It's even worse when there are no children around. Because the childish adult replaces the child. Coupled life and family life bring out everything that's childish in everyone involved. Why do they have to sleep night after night in the same bed? Why must they be on the phone to each other five times a day? Why are they always *with* each other? The forced deference is certainly childish. That unnatural deference. In one of the magazines, I read recently about a famous media couple married thirty-four years and the marvelous achievement of their learning to bear each other. Proudly the husband told the reporter, "My wife and I have a saying that you can tell the health of a marriage by the number of teeth marks on your tongue." I wonder, when I'm around such people, What are they being punished for? Thirty-four years. One stands in awe of the masochistic rigor required.

I have a friend in Austin, a very successful writer. Married young in the mid-1950s, then in the early seventies got divorced. Married to a decent woman with whom he produced three decent children—and he wanted out. And he didn't get out hysterically or foolishly. It was a human rights issue. Give me liberty or give me death. Well, after the divorce he went off to live alone and at liberty and he was miserable. And so within a short time he married again, a woman this time with whom he didn't plan to have any children, who already had a college-age child of her own. A married life *without* children. Well, sex had to be over in a couple of years, yet this is a man who was vigorously adulterous throughout his first marriage and focused on sex in his writing. On his own he could have begun to enjoy openly all that he finagled surreptitiously while married. Yet unsprung from his constraints, he's miserable from the first second and believes that he'll be miserable forever. He is at liberty in the face of the fullness, and he has no idea where he is. All he knows to do is to find his way back into the condition he could no longer stand, though now without the compelling logic of wanting to be married so as to have children, to raise a family, et cetera. The charm of the surreptitious? I don't disparage it. Marriage at its best is a sure-fire stimulant to the thrills of licentious subterfuge. But my friend's need was for something more basic to his safety than the adulterer's daily drama of fording a river of lies. That wasn't the kick he remarried for, even though once he was a husband again he almost immediately resumed pursuing the old delights. Part of the problem is that emancipated manhood never has had a social spokesman or an educational system. It has no social status because people don't want it to have social status. Yet this fellow's circumstances so favored living to the limit of his prerogatives, if only for the dignity of it. But deferring, deferring, deferring? Appeasing, appeasing, appeasing? Every other day dreaming of leaving? No, it's not a dignified way to be a man. Or, I told Elena, to be a woman.

Was she persuaded? I don't know. I don't think so. Aren't you? Why, why are you laughing? What's so hilarious? My didacticism? I agree: one's absurd side is never unimpressive. But what can be done about it? I'm a critic, I'm a teacher—didacticism is my destiny. Argument and counterargument is what history's made of. One either imposes one's ideas or one is imposed on. Like it or not, that's the predicament. There are always opposing forces, and so, unless one is inordinately fond of subordination, one is always at war.

Look, I'm not of this age. You can see that. You can hear that. I achieved my goal with a blunt instrument. I took a hammer to domestic life and those who stand watch over it. And to Kenny's life. That I'm still a hammerer should be no surprise. Nor is it a surprise that my insistence makes me a comic figure on the order of the village atheist to you who are of the current age and who haven't had to insist on any of this.

Now, let the laughter subside and allow teacher to finish. To be sure, if pleasure, experience, and age is a subject of interest no longer . . . It is? Then make what you'll make of me, but not till the end.

This past Christmas. Christmas 1999. I dreamt of Consuela that night. I was alone and I dreamt that something was happening to her and I thought I should call her. But when I looked in the telephone directory, she was no longer there, and because under George's tutelage I wouldn't allow myself to renew the agitation that could have destroyed me, I had never written down that Upper East Side address I'd found in the phone book years earlier, after she got her first job. Well, a week later, on New Year's Eve, I was alone in my living room, without a girl, purposely by myself that night playing my piano because I intended to ignore the millennial celebration. Providing you're not in a state of longing, living in solitude can be its own powerful pleasure, and it was that pleasure I was planning on that night. My answering machine was on, and even normally I don't pick up the receiver when the phone rings but just listen to see who it is. That night particularly I was determined to hear not one word from anyone about "Y2K," and so when the phone does ring, I go right on with my playing until I realize that it's her voice I'm hearing. "Hello, David? It's me. It's Consuela. It's a long time since we spoke, it's strange to phone you, but I want to tell you something. And I want to tell it to you myself, before you hear it from someone. Or before you hear it by surprise. I'll be phoning you again. But here's my cell phone number."

I listened to the message, frozen. I didn't pick up the receiver, and then when I did go for it, it was too late, and I thought, Oh God, something *has* happened to her. It was because of George's death that I imagined the worst for Consuela. Yes, George died. You didn't see the obit in the *Times*? George O'Hearn died five months ago. I'm without my closest male friend. I'm now virtually without any male friend. It's a big loss, the camaraderie with George. I have colleagues, sure, people I see at work and talk to in passing, but the assumptions underlying the way they live are so antithetical to mine that it's difficult for us ever to think freely together. We have no common language about personal life. George was the whole of my male community, perhaps because the class of men we belong to is small to begin with. And a single comrade-in-arms is sufficient: one doesn't need the whole of society on one's side. I find that most other men I know—especially if they happen to have run into me with one of my young girls—either silently judge me or openly preach to me. I am "a limited man," they tell me—they who are not limited. And the preachers can get mad when I don't recognize the truth of their argument. I am "smug," they tell me—they who are not smug. The tortured ones, of course, don't want any part of me. Certainly none of the married men ever open up to me. With them there is no affinity whatsoever. Maybe they reserve their confidences for one another, though I wonder—I don't know that male solidarity extends very far these days. Their heroism is not only in stoically enduring the dailiness of their renunciations but in diligently presenting a counterfeit image of their lives. The true lives, the unhidden lives, exist for their therapists alone. I'm not contending that they're all antagonistic and wish me ill because of the way I live, but it's safe to say that I don't universally compel admiration. With George dead, my solidarity is now entirely with women like Elena who once were girlfriends. They can't offer what I had with George, but I don't appear to make an excessive demand on their tolerance.

His age? George was fifty-five. A stroke. He had a

stroke. I was there when he had it. So were some eight hundred others. It was at the Ninety-second Street Y. A Saturday night in September. He was about to give a reading. I was the one at the lectern introducing him. He was sitting in a chair just off-stage, in the wings, enjoying my introduction and nodding approval. Stretched out in front of him, in his narrow mortician's suit, were those long, lean legs of his—pliable George, in his suit, was a wire coat-hanger of a hook-nosed black Irishman. Apparently he had the stroke while he was sitting there with his six books of verse stacked up in his lap, waiting to come on, in lugubrious black, and charm the bejesus out of the crowd. Because when the audience began to applaud and he went to get up, he just tumbled out of the chair and it fell on top of him. Casting his oeuvre all over the floor. The doctors never thought he'd leave the hospital. But he hung on there uncon-scious for a week, and then the family took him home to die.

He was mostly unconscious at home, too. His left side paralyzed. Vocal cords paralyzed. A big chunk of his brain, just blown. His son Tom's a physician, and he oversaw the dying, which required another nine days. Took him off the IV, removed the catheter, took him off everything. Whenever George opened his eyes, they propped him up and gave him water to sip and ice to suck on. Otherwise they kept him as comfortable as they could while he slipped away at an agonizingly slow pace.

Every afternoon, at the end of the day, I drove to Pelham to see him. George had sequestered the family in Pelham so that, during all those years when he was teaching at the New School, he could have a free hand in Manhattan. There were sometimes as many as five or six cars parked in the drive when I arrived. The children were there in shifts, sometimes with one or the other of the grandchildren. There was a nurse and, near the end, the hospice person. Kate, George's wife, was, of course, there round the clock. I'd go into the bedroom, where they'd installed a hospital bed, and I'd take his hand, the hand on the side where he could still feel something, and I'd sit with him for fifteen, twenty minutes, but he was always out of it. Heavy breathing. Moaning. The good leg twitching once in a while, but nothing more. Pass my hand over his hair, touch his cheek, squeeze his fingers, but no response. I sat there hoping that he might come around and recognize me, and then I drove home. Then one afternoon I showed up and they said it had happened—he was awake. Go in, go in, they said.

They had George propped up on pillows and the bed half raised. His daughter Betty was feeding him ice. She was cracking slivers of ice between her teeth and putting the broken little bits into his mouth. George was trying to chomp on them with the teeth on the side of his mouth that still worked. He looked far gone indeed, *so* thin, but his eyes were open, and there he was, employing all that remained of his concentration in order to chew that ice. Kate stood in the doorway watching him, an imposing white-haired woman nearly as tall as George, but bulkier than when I'd seen her last, and far wearier. Attractively roundish, wry, resilient, radiating a kind of stubborn heartiness—that was Kate well into her middle years. A woman never known to shrink from reality, who looked now completely worn down, as if she'd fought her last battle and lost.

Tom brought a wet washcloth from the bathroom. "Want to freshen up, Dad?" he said. "How much does he know?" I asked Tom. "How much does he understand?" "There are stretches," Tom said, "when he seems to know something. And then he doesn't." "How long has he been awake?" "About half an hour. Go over to him. Speak to him, David. He seems to enjoy the voices."

Enjoy? Strange word. But Tom, in all situations, is the jovial doctor. I came around to George's unparalyzed side while Tom was mopping his father's face with the wet washcloth. George took it from him—to everyone's surprise, reached out with his good hand, grabbed at the washcloth, got hold of it, and jammed it inside his mouth. "He's so dry," somebody said. George pushed the end of the washcloth around inside his mouth and began to suck on it. When he took it out, there was something adhering to it. Looked like a piece of his soft palate. Betty let out a gasp when she saw it there, and the hospice woman, who was in the room too, patted Betty's back and said, "It's nothing. His mouth is so dry—it's just a little flake of flesh."

His mouth was aslant, hanging open, that stricken-looking mouth of the dying, but his eyes were focused and there even appeared to be something back of them, something of George that hadn't yet given way. Like the wall left jaggedly standing after a bomb goes off. With the same angry force with which he'd grabbed the washcloth, he pulled down the sheet that was covering him and began to yank at the Velcro at the corner of his diaper, trying to pull the thing off, and revealing those sad sticks that had been his legs. When the tungsten filament inside a light bulb goes—that's what his legs reminded me of. Everything about him, everything fashioned of flesh and blood, reminded me of an inanimate something else. "No, no," Tom said, "let it be, Dad. It's fine." But George wouldn't stop. Pulling angrily, trying in vain to get out of the diaper. When that didn't work, he raised his hand and, kind of growling, pointed at Betty. "What?" she asked him. "I can't understand you. What do you want? What is it, sweetheart?" The noises he was emitting were indecipherable, but it was clear from his gestures that he wanted her to come as close as she could. When she did, he reached out, put his arm around onto her back, and pulled her forward so that he could kiss her mouth. "Oh yes, Daddy," she said, "yes, you are the best father, the very best." What was astonishing was this force welling up in him after all those days of lying there inert and emaciated, somehow hanging on while seemingly breathing his last—the considerable force with which he'd pulled Betty to him and with which he was trying to speak. Maybe, I thought, they shouldn't be letting him die. What if there's more left than they realize? What if that's what he's trying to demonstrate? What if instead of saying goodbye to them he's saying, "Don't let me go. Do everything you can to save me"?

Then George was pointing at me. "Hello, George," I said. "Hello, friend. It's David, George." And when I got close to him, he grabbed me the way he'd grabbed Betty and kissed *me* on the mouth.

There was no necrotic smell, no sickish stink, no stench whatsoever: just the warm, odorless breath, the pure perfume of being, and the two parched lips. It was the first time George and I had ever kissed in our lives. Again the grunting and he was pointing now to Tom. To Tom and then to his own feet, which were uncovered at the end of the bed. When Tom, thinking George wanted the sheet pulled up over his legs, began to straighten the bedding, George grunted still louder and pointed again at his feet. "He wants you to hold them," Betty said. "One of them he can't even feel," Tom said. "Hold the other one," Betty said. "Okay, Dad, I've got it—I've got you." And Tom began patiently kneading the foot in which there was feeling.

Next George pointed to the doorway where Kate was standing, watching it all. "He wants you, Ma," Betty said. I moved aside and Kate came over and stood where I'd been, beside the bed, and George reached up for her now, and with his good arm pulled her toward him, and kissed her as forcefully as he'd kissed Betty and me. Kate kissed him back. Then they kissed again, a long kiss this time, a quite passionate kiss. Kate even closed her eyes. She's an exceedingly unsentimental, down-to-earth person, and I'd never before seen her do anything so girlish.

Meanwhile, George's good hand had moved from

her back around to her right arm, and he began to fumble with the button at the wrist of her blouse. He was trying to undo it. "George," Kate whispered softly. She sounded amused. "Georgie, Georgie . . ." "Help him, Ma. He wants to open the button." Smiling at the instructions from the emotional daughter, Kate submitted and opened the button, but by then George was at the other sleeve, tugging at *that* button, so she obligingly undid it as well. And all this time he kept hungrily going for her lips. Kate caressed his ruined face, that immensely lonely, cavernous face, kissed his lips each time he offered them, and then his hand went up to the buttons at the front of her blouse and he began to fumble with those.

His plan was clear: he was trying to undress her. To undress this woman whom, as I knew, as the children surely knew, he had not touched in bed in years. Whom he barely any longer touched at all. "Let him, Ma," Betty said, and so Kate again did as her daughter told her. She reached up with her own hand and helped George undo the front of her blouse. This time when they kissed, his one good hand was grasping at the cloth of her large brassiere. But, abruptly, that was the end of it. The force went out of him just like that, and he never reached her pendulous breasts. He didn't die for another twelve hours, but when he fell back onto the pillows, his mouth agape, his eyes closed, breathing like one who's collapsed at the end of a race, we all knew that what we had witnessed was the last amazing act of George's life.

Later, when I went to the door to leave, Kate came out onto the front porch and continued with me down the drive to my car. She took my hands in hers and thanked me for coming. I said, "I was glad I was here to see all this." "Yes, that was something, wasn't it?" Kate said. And then with her weary smile she added, "I wonder who it is he thought I was."

So George was only five months gone, and when Consuela called and left her message—"I want to tell you something. And I want to tell it to you myself, before you hear it from someone"—well, as I said, I listened to the message thinking something had now happened to *her*. This kind of thing, a premonitory dream followed by its fulfillment, is uncanny enough *in* one's dreams, but in real life? I didn't know what to do. Should I call her back? I thought it over for fifteen minutes. I didn't call back because I was afraid to. Why does she phone me? What can it be? My life is untroubled and back in my hands. Have I the resilience for Consuela and her aggressive yielding? I am no longer sixty-two—I am seventy. Can I endure at this age that mania of uncertainty? Do I dare relapse into that frenzied trance? Can that possibly be good for my longevity?

I remembered how for the three years after I lost her, even when I got up in the dark to take a leak, she was all I thought about: even at four A.M., standing over the toilet seven-eighths asleep, the Kepesh one-eighth awake would begin to mutter her name. Generally when an old man pisses at night, his mind is completely blank. If he's capable of thinking of anything, it's only about getting back into bed. But not me, not then. "Consuela, Consuela, Consuela," every single time I got up to go. And she'd done this to me, mind you, without language, without cogitation, without cunning, without an ounce of malevolence, and with no regard to cause and effect. Like a great athlete or a work of idealized sculptural art or an animal glimpsed in the woods, like Michael Jordan, like a Maillol, like an owl, like a bobcat, she'd done it through the simplicity of physical splendor. There was nothing the least bit sadistic in Consuela. Not even the sadism of indifference, which often goes with that magnitude of perfection. She was too square for such cruelty and far too kind. But imagine the sport she could have made of me were she not

too well reared a girl ever to exploit to the limit
the Amazonian strength of her endowment; imagine
if she'd had Amazonian consciousness as well and
Machiavellianly grasped the impact she had. Luck-
ily, like most people, she was not practiced in thinking things through, and though she made the whole
thing between us happen, she never understood all
that happened. If she did, and if, in addition, she'd
had the tiniest taste for tormenting the male who's
on fire, I would have been a goner, wrecked entirely
by my own White Whale.

But here she was again. No, absolutely no! Never
again that assault on my peace of mind!

But then I thought, She's looking for me, she
needs me, and not as a lover, not as a teacher, not so
as to resume our erotic tale with a new installment.
So I rang her cell phone and lied and said I went
to the store and just got back, and she said, "I'm in
the car. I was in front of your building when I left
the message." I said, "What are you doing driving
around New York on New Year's Eve?" "I don't
know what I'm doing," she said. "Are you crying,
Consuela?" "No, not yet." And I said, "Did you ring
the doorbell?" She said, "No, I didn't, because I
didn't dare to." "You can always ring the bell, always.
You know that. What's the matter?" "I need you

now." "Then come." "Do you have time?" "I always have time for you. Come." "There's something important. I'm coming right away."

I put down the receiver and I didn't know what to expect. About twenty minutes later, a car stopped, and the moment I opened the door for her I knew something had gone wrong. Because she had a cap on her head like a fez. And that wasn't something she would wear. She has dark black hair, sleek hair that was always cared for, always washed, brushed, combed; she would see the hairdresser every two weeks. But now she was standing there with a fez on her head. She also had a stylish coat on, a belted black Persian lamb coat nearly to the floor, and when she undid the belt, I saw underneath her coat the silk shirt with the cleavage—lovely. So I embraced her and she embraced me, and she let me take her coat, and I said, "Your hat? Your fez?" and she said, "You'd better not do that. The surprise will be too great." I said, "Why?" And she said, "Because I'm very ill."

We went into the living room, and there again I embraced her, and she pushed her body to me, and you feel the tits, the beautiful tits, and you see over her shoulder the beautiful buttocks. You see the beautiful body. She's now in her thirties, thirty-two, and not less but more lovely, and the face, which seems somehow to have lengthened a bit, is far more womanly—and she's telling me, "I don't have any hair anymore. In October I was told that I've got cancer. I've got breast cancer." I said, "This is awful, this is horrible, how do you feel, how does one deal with such a thing?" Her chemotherapy had begun in early November, and quickly she'd lost her hair. She said, "I have to tell you the story," and we sat down and I said, "Tell me everything." "Well, my aunt, my mother's sister, has had breast cancer, and she was treated for it, and she lost a breast. So I knew that in my family there's danger. I always knew this, and I've always been afraid of it," and all the time she was talking, I was thinking, You, with the most gorgeous tits in the world. And she said, "One morning I was standing under the shower, and I felt something under my armpit, and I knew that this was wrong. I went to my doctor and he said it's probably nothing to worry about, and so I went to a second doctor and a third doctor, you know the story, and the third doctor said it *was* something to worry about." "And did you panic?" I asked her. "Did you panic, my lovely friend?" I was so shaken, *I* was panicking. "Yes," she said, "enormously." "At night?" "Yes, I was running around my apartment. I was completely crazy." I started to cry when I heard this, and we were embracing again, and I said, "Why didn't you call me? Why didn't you call me then?" And she said again, "I didn't dare." And I said, "Whom did you think of to call?" And she said, "My mother, of course. But I knew she'd panic too, because I'm her daughter, her one and only daughter, and because she's so emotional, and because everyone has died. David, they're all dead." "Who has died?" "My father is dead." "How?" "His plane crashed. He was on that plane to Paris. He was going for business." "Oh, no." "Yes." "And the grandfather you loved so much?" "He died. Six years ago. It began with losing him. A heart attack." "And your grandmother, with her rosaries? The grandmother who was the duchess?" "She died too. After him. She was old and she died." "Not your kid brother—?" "No, no, he's fine. But I couldn't call him, I couldn't about this. He couldn't handle this. That's when I thought of you. But I didn't know if you were alone." "That's not a problem. Promise me now one thing. If you should start to panic during the night, during the day, any-time, phone me. I'll always come. Here," I said, "write down your address. Write down all your phone numbers, work, home, everything." And I was thinking, She is dying before my eyes, she too is now dying. Instability had merely to enter her cozy

Cuban family life with the predictable death of a beloved old grandfather to set rapidly in motion a cascade of misfortune culminating in cancer.

I said, "Are you afraid right now?" And she said, "Very. Very much afraid. I'm all right for two minutes, I'm thinking of something else, and then the bottom falls out of my stomach and I can't believe what's happening. It's a roller coaster, and it doesn't stop. It can't stop unless the *cancer* stops. My chances," she said, "are sixty percent to survive and forty percent to die." And then she dropped into the talk about how life is so worthwhile and how she feels sorry for her mother, above all—the banal talk that's inevitable. I wanted to do so many things, I had so many plans, and so on. She began telling me about how foolish all her little anxieties of a few months back now seemed, the worries about work and friends and clothes, and how this had put everything in perspective, and I thought, No, nothing puts anything in perspective.

I was watching her, listening to her, and when I couldn't hear any more, I said, "Do you mind if I touch your breasts?" She said, "No, go ahead." "You don't mind?" "No. I do mind kissing you, though. Because I don't want anything sexual. But I do know how much you like my breasts, so touch my breasts."

So I touched them—and with trembling hands. And of course with an erection. I said, "Is it your left breast or your right breast?" and she said, "It's my right breast." So I put my hand on her right breast. There is a combination of eroticism and tenderness, and it melts you and arouses you, and that's what was happening. You get a hard-on and melt, both at the same time. So we're sitting there with her breast in my hand, and we're talking, and I said, "You don't mind?" And she said, "I even want more of you. Because I know you love my breasts." I said, "What do you want?" "I want you to feel my cancer." I said, "I'll do that. Okay. But later, we'll do that later on."

It was too soon. I wasn't ready for that. So we talked, and *she* started to cry, and I tried to comfort her, and then suddenly she stopped crying and became very energetic, very determined. She said to me, "David, I came to you, in fact, with only one request, one question." And I said, "What is it?" And she said, "After you, I never had a boyfriend or a lover who loved my body as much as you loved it." "Have you had boyfriends?"

At it again. Forget about the boyfriends. But I couldn't. "Have you, Consuela? "Yes, but not many." "Have you slept with men regularly?" "No. Not on a regular basis." "How was your job? Was there nobody at your job who fell in love with you?" "They all did." "I can understand that. But then what," I said. "Were they all gay? Didn't you meet straight men?" "I do, I did, but they're no good." "Why are they no good?" "They're just masturbating on my body." "Well, this is a pity. This is stupid. This is insane." "But you loved my body. And I was proud of it." "But you were proud of it before." "Yes and no. You've seen my body at its most glorious. So I wanted you to see it before it is ruined by what the doctors are going to do." "Stop talking that way, don't think that way. Nobody's going to ruin you. What do the doctors say they're going to do?" And she said, "I've had chemotherapy. That's why I don't take off my cap." "Of course. But where you're concerned, I can stand anything. Do whatever you want." She said, "No, I don't want to show it to you. Because a strange thing happens to your hair. After the chemotherapy, it starts to come out in hand-fuls. A sort of baby hair begins growing on your head. It's very strange." I asked, "Does your pubic hair disappear?" "No," she said, "it doesn't, it stays. Which is strange too." I said, "Did you ask the doc-tor?" "Yes," she said, "and the doctor can't explain it. She only answered, 'That's a good question.' Look at my arms," Consuela said. She has long, slender arms and that white-white skin, and the fine lovely hair on her arms was indeed still there. "Look," she said, "there's hair on my arms but not on my head." "Well," I said, "I've known bald men, so why can't I see a bald woman?" She said, "No. I don't want you to see."

Then she said, "David, may I ask you a big favor?" "Of course. Anything." "Would you mind saying goodbye to my breasts?" I said, "My dear girl, my darling girl, they're not going to demolish your body, they're not." "Well, I'm lucky that I have so much breast, but they're going to have to take out about a third. My doctor's trying everything to keep the surgery minimal. She's humane. She's wonderful. She's not a butcher. She's not a heartless machine. She's trying first to shrink the cancer with chemo. Then when they operate they can take out as little as possible." "But they can restore it, rebuild it, can't they, whatever it is they take out?" "Yes, they can put in some silicone stuff. But I don't know if I'll want it. Because this is my body and that won't be my body. That won't be anything." "And how do you want me to say goodbye? What do you want? What are you asking me, Consuela?" And at last she told me.

I got my camera, which is a Leica with a zoom lens, and she stood up. We closed the curtains, we put on all the lights, I found the right Schubert and put that on, and she didn't quite dance then, but it was, rather, an exotic, Oriental sort of movement when she started to undress. Very elegant and so vulnerable. I was sitting on the sofa, and she was standing and undressing. And the way in which she undressed and dropped each item, it was spellbinding. Mata Hari. The spy undressing for the officer. And all the time so extremely vulnerable. She took off her blouse first. Then her shoes. Extraordinary to take off her shoes then. Then she took off her bra. And it was as though a man who had undressed had forgotten to pull his socks off, which makes him look slightly ludicrous. A woman in a skirt with naked breasts is not erotic to me. The skirt somehow confuses the picture. Naked breasts with trousers is very erotic, but over just a skirt it doesn't work. You'd be better off to keep on your bra with a skirt, but a skirt alone with naked breasts is to feed somebody.

So she showed herself to me. She undressed until she had only the panties on. She said, "Could you touch my breasts?" "Is that the picture you want, my touching them?" "No, no. Touch them first." So I did. And then she said, "I want pictures facing the camera, and in profile, and then hanging over."

I took about thirty pictures of her. She chose the poses, and she wanted everything. She wanted to have her hands underneath, holding them. She wanted to be squeezing them. She wanted them from the left side, from the right side, she wanted them photographed while she was bending forward. Finally she pulled off her panties, and you could see that her pubic hair was there as it had always been, as I described it: sleek, lying flat. Asian hair. She appeared to be all at once aroused by taking off her panties and my looking at her with nothing on. That happened suddenly. You could see by her nipples that she was aroused. Though by now I no longer was. Still, I asked her, "Do you want to stay for the night? Do you want to sleep with me?" She said, "No. I don't want to sleep with you. I want to be in your arms, though." I was fully dressed, as I am now. And she was sitting on the sofa in my arms, very close to me, and then she took my wrist and she laid my hand on her armpit in order for me to feel the cancer. Felt like a stone. A stone in the armpit. Two small stones, one bigger than the other, meaning that there is a metastasis originating in her breast. But you couldn't feel it in her breast. I asked, "Why can't I feel it in your breast?" and she said, "My breasts are too big. There's too much tissue to feel it. It's deep inside the breast."

I couldn't have slept with her, not even I who'd licked the blood from her. After the years of dwelling on her, just seeing her would have been difficult enough had she shown up under normal circumstances and not in this bizarrely wretched way. So, no, I couldn't have slept with her, and yet I kept thinking about it. Because they're so beautiful, her breasts. I cannot say it often enough. It was so mean, so degrading, these breasts, her breasts—I just thought, They can't be destroyed! As I told you, I'd been masturbating over her without interruption during all the years we were apart. I have been in bed with other women, and I have thought of her, of her breasts, of what it was like with my face sinking into them. Thought of their softness, their smoothness, the way I could sense their weight, their soft weight, and this while my mouth nuzzles somebody else. But at that moment I knew hers was no longer a sexual life. What was at stake was something else.

So I said to her, "Should I go with you to the hospital? I'll do that if you want me to. I insist on doing it. You're virtually alone." She said she wanted to think about it. She said, "It's sweet of you to offer, but I don't know yet. I don't know if I'll want to see you immediately after I've been operated on." She left about half past one; she'd arrived about eight o'clock. She didn't ask what I was going to do with the photographs she'd wanted me to take. She didn't ask me to send her prints. I haven't had them developed yet. I'm curious to see them. I'll enlarge them. I'll send her a set, of course. But I'll have to find somebody I trust to develop them. I should long ago, with my interests, have learned how to develop film myself, but I never did. It would have been useful.

She should be going to the hospital any time now. I'm expecting a message from her any moment, any day. Since I saw her three weeks ago, I haven't heard a word. Will I? Do you think I will? She told me not to contact her. She didn't want anything more from me—that's what she said when she left. I've been all but keeping a vigil by the phone for fear of missing her call.

Ever since her visit, I've myself been on the phone to people I know, to doctors I know, trying to find out about breast cancer treatment. Because I had always understood that the procedure for this sort of thing was surgery first and then the chemotherapy. And that was worrying me while she was here—I kept thinking, There's something about her case I'm failing to understand. Now I learn that giving chemo before isn't entirely unheard of, that it's becoming the standard of care for treatment of locally advanced breast cancer, but the question is, apparently, is that the treatment right for her? What did she mean

about sixty percent chance of survival? Why only
sixty? Did someone tell her that or did she read it
somewhere or, in her panic, did she make it up? Or
are they gambling with long-term survival for pur-
poses of vanity? Maybe this is merely a response to
the shock—a typical enough response at that—but I
can't stop thinking that there's something about her
story, either that she didn't tell me or that she herself
hasn't been told . . . Anyway, that was the story, as I
got it, and I haven't as yet heard any more.

She left me at about one-thirty A.M., after the New
Year reached Chicago. We had some tea. We drank a
glass of wine. Because she asked me to, I turned on
the television, and we watched the replay of the New
Year beginning in Australia and sweeping across Asia
and Europe. She was slightly sentimental. Telling
stories. About her childhood. About her father taking her to the opera since she was a little girl. She
told a story about a florist. "I was buying flowers on
Madison Avenue with my mother last Saturday," she
told me, "and the florist said, 'What a nice hat you're
wearing,' and I said, 'It's there for a purpose,' and he
understood, and he blushed and apologized and gave
me a dozen roses for free. So there you see how
people respond to a human being in distress. They

don't know what to do. Nobody knows what to say or to do. So I'm very grateful to you," she said.

How did I feel? The greatest pain I felt that night was over her being alone and panicking in her bed. Panicking about death. And what will happen now? What do you think? I guess she's not going to ask me to go with her to the hospital. She was pleased that I offered to, but when the time comes, she'll go to the hospital with her mother. She may just have gone berserk New Year's Eve because she was too miserable and frightened to go to the party where she'd been invited and too miserable and frightened to be alone. I don't think she will phone me when she's in a panic. She wanted the offer, but she won't use it.

Unless I'm wrong. Unless two or three months from now she comes to me and says she wants to sleep with me. With me rather than a younger man because I'm old and far from perfect myself. With me because, though still this side of desiccation, the decomposing corpse is no longer quite so well concealed as it is with the men at my gym who managed not to be born before Roosevelt took office.

And will I be able to do it? In all my years, I've never slept with a woman who has been mutilated in this manner. I can speak only of one woman I knew some years ago, and on the way to my apartment, she said, "I have to tell you—because of an operation, I've only got one breast. So I don't want you to be shocked by it." Now, no matter how unflinching you like to think you are, if you're honest about it, the prospect of seeing a woman with one breast is not very inviting, is it? I was able to act a little surprised, but seemingly not about the one breast, and I don't think I exhibited my nervousness at trying to put her at her ease. "Oh, don't be silly, we're not going there to sleep together. We're just good friends and I think we should stay good friends." I once slept with a woman who had a dark brownish wine stain— between her breasts and partly over her breasts, a huge birthmark. This woman was also a tall woman. Six five. The only woman I've ever had to kiss by standing on my toes and craning my neck. I got a crick in the neck from kissing her. When we went to bed, she started to undress by pulling off her skirt and her panties, which women normally don't do. They usually take off the blouse first, they start to undress their upper body. But she kept on her sweater and her bra. I said, "Aren't you going to take off your bra and your sweater?" "Yes, but I don't want you to be surprised." She said, "There's something wrong with me." I smiled, tried to make light of it. "Tell me, what is wrong?" She said, "Well, there's something about my breasts that will shock you." "Oh, don't worry. Show me." And so she did. And I started overdoing things. Kissing the birth-mark. Touching it. Playing with it. Being polite. Making her feel happy with it. Saying I loved it. Such things aren't easy to take in stride. But you're supposed to be able to take charge, to act unhysteri-cally, to deal with such things with grace. Not to recoil from anything that a body must abide. That wine stain. It was tragic for her. Six foot five. Men drawn to her, as I was, by this amazing height. And with every man, the same story: "There's something wrong with me."

The photographs. I'll never forget Consuela ask-ing me to take those pictures. To some Peeping Tom peering in from outside, it could only have looked like a scene from pornography. Yet it was as far as you could get from pornography. "Do you have your camera?" "I have my camera," I said. "Would you mind taking pictures of me? Because I want to have pictures of my body as you knew it. As you saw it. Because soon it won't be as it was. I don't know anybody else I could ask to do this. I couldn't ask this of another man. Otherwise I wouldn't have bothered you." "Yes," I told her, "we'll do this. Anything. Say what you want. Ask for whatever you want. Say everything to me." "Could you put on some music," she said, "and then get your camera?" "What music do you want?" I asked. "Schubert. Some Schubert chamber music." "Okay, okay," I said, but not, I told myself, *Death and the Maiden.*

Yet she hasn't asked me to send her a print. Remember that Consuela is not the most brilliant girl in the world. Because then the photographs would be another story. Then there would be tactics involved. Then her strategy would be something to think about. But with Consuela, there's a semiconscious spontaneity in whatever she does, a rightness, though she may not know quite what she's doing or exactly why. Coming to me to be photographed, that's very close to nature, to an original drifting thought, to intuition, and there is no deliberate reasoning behind it. You could make up the reasoning, but Consuela wouldn't have. She feels she has to do this, she says, to document for *me*, who loved her body so much, the quality it had, how perfect it was. But there was much more to it than that.

I've noticed that most women are unsure about their bodies, even if, like her, they are altogether lovely. Not all of them know they're lovely. It takes a certain type of woman to know that. Most have complaints about something that they needn't complain about. They often want to hide their breasts. There's some shame whose source I can never fathom, and you must reassure them for a long time before they expose them with any real pleasure and take real pleasure in being looked at. Even the most fortunate of them. There are only a few who show themselves freely, and these days, because of all the polemicizing, they're often not the ones with the model of breast you would have invented yourself.

But the erotic power of Consuela's body—well, that is over. Yes, that night I'd had an erection, but I couldn't have sustained it. I'm fortunate enough to have a hard-on and the drive, but I would have been in great trouble if she had asked me to sleep with her that night. I'll be in great trouble when she asks me once she is recovered from the surgery. As she will. Because she will, won't she? Try it out first with someone familiar and someone old. For the sake of her confidence, for the sake of her pride, better with me than with Carlos Alonso or the Villareal boys. Age may not do what cancer does, but it does enough.

Part Two. She asks me three months from now, she calls me and says, "Let's get together," and then she takes her clothes off again. Is that the disaster to come?

There's a painting of Stanley Spencer's that hangs

at the Tate, a double nude portrait of Spencer and his wife in their middle forties. It is the quintessence of directness about cohabitation, about the sexes living together over time. It's in one of the Spencer books downstairs. I'll get it later. Spencer is seated, squatting, beside the recumbent wife. He is looking ruminatively down at her from close range through his wire-rimmed glasses. We, in turn, are looking at them from close range: two naked bodies right in our faces, the better for us to see how they are no longer young and attractive. Neither is happy. There is a heavy past clinging to the present. For the wife particularly, everything has begun to slacken, to thicken, and greater rigors than striating flesh are to come.

At the edge of a table, in the immediate foreground of the picture, are two pieces of meat, a large leg of lamb and a single small chop. The raw meat is rendered with physiological meticulousness, with the same uncharitable candor as the sagging breasts and the pendent, unaroused prick displayed only inches back from the uncooked food. You could be looking through the butcher's window, not just at the meat but at the sexual anatomy of the married couple. Every time I think of Consuela, I envision that raw leg of lamb shaped like a primitive club beside the blatantly exhibited bodies of this husband and wife. Its being there, so close to their mattress, becomes less and less incongruous the longer you look. There's melancholy resignation in the somewhat stunned expression of the wife, and there is that butchered hunk of meat having nothing in common with a living lamb, and, for three weeks now, ever since Consuela's visit, I can get neither image out of my mind.

We watched the New Year coming in around the world, the mass hysteria of no significance that was the millennial New Year's Eve celebration. Brilliance flaring across the time zones, and none ignited by bin Laden. Light whirling over nighttime London more spectacular than anything since the splendors of colored smoke billowed up from the Blitz. And the Eiffel Tower shooting fire, a facsimile flame-throwing weapon such as Wernher von Braun might have designed for Hitler's annihilating arsenal—the historical missile of missiles, the rocket of rockets, the bomb of bombs, with ancient Paris the launching pad and the whole of humanity the target. All evening long, on networks everywhere, the mockery of the Armageddon that we'd been awaiting in our backyard shelters since August 6, 1945. How could it not happen? Even on that very night, especially on that night, people anticipating the worst as though the evening were one long air-raid drill. The wait for the chain of horrendous Hiroshimas to link in synchronized destruction the abiding civilizations of the world. It's now or never. And it never came.

Maybe that's what everyone was celebrating—that it hadn't come, never came, that the disaster of the end will now never arrive. All the disorder is controlled disorder punctuated with intervals to sell automobiles. TV doing what it does best: the triumph of trivialization over tragedy. The Triumph of the Surface, with Barbara Walters. Rather than the destruction of the age-old cities, an international eruption of the superficial instead, a global outbreak of sentimentality such as even Americans hadn't witnessed before. From Sydney to Bethlehem to Times Square, the recirculating of clichés occurs at supersonic speeds. No bombs go off, no blood is shed— the next bang you hear will be the boom of prosperity and the explosion of markets. The slightest lucidity about the misery made ordinary by our era sedated by the grandiose stimulation of the grandest illusion. Watching this hyped-up production of staged pandemonium, I have a sense of the monied world eagerly entering the prosperous dark ages. A night of human happiness to usher in barbarism.com. To welcome appropriately the shit and the kitsch of the new millennium. A night not to re-member but to forget.

Except on the sofa where I sit holding Consuela, my arms encircling her where she is naked, warm-ing her breasts with my hands while we watch New Year's Eve arrive in Cuba. Neither of us had been expecting *that* to materialize on the screen, but there before us is Havana. From an amphitheater cor-ralling a thousand tourists and calling itself a night-club comes an embalmed police-state embodiment of the Caribbean hot stuff that used to draw the big spenders in the days of the Mob. The Tropicana Nightclub of the Tropicana Hotel. No Cubans to be seen other than the entertainers in no way entertain-ing, a lot of young people—ninety-six of them, ABC says—wearing silly white costumes and not so much dancing or singing as circling the stage howling in-to hand-held mikes. The showgirls look like leggy Latino West Village transvestites walking around in a huff. Atop their heads are overdeveloped lamp-shades—three feet high, according to ABC. Lamp-shades on their heads and a rippling great mane of white ruffles down their backs.

"My God," Consuela said, and she began to cry. "This," she said, and so angrily, "*this* is what he gives the world. This is what he shows them on New Year's

Eve." "It *is* a bit of a grotesque farce. Maybe," I said, "it's Castro's idea of a joke."

Is it, I wonder. Is this unconscious self-satire—is Castro so out of touch—or is it intentionally satirical and consistent with his hatred of the capitalist world? Castro, so contemptuous of the Batista corruption, corruption that you would have thought to be symbolized for him by tourist nightclubs like this Tropicana, and that is his millennial offering? The pope wouldn't do this—he has great public relations. Only the old Soviet Union could have equaled the tawdriness. There are any number of things for Castro to choose from, any number of old-fashioned socialist-realism tableaux: a celebration at a sugar plantation, in a maternity ward, at a cigar factory. Happy Cuban workers smoking, happy Cuban mothers beaming, happy Cuban newborns nursing . . . but to present the crappiest sort of entertainment for tourists? Was it deliberate or stupid or was it thought to be an appropriate joke on all this hysterical celebrating over a meaningless mark on the historical grid? Whatever the motive, he will not spend a dime on it. He will not spend a minute thinking about it. Why should Castro the revolutionary care, why should anyone care, about something that gives us a sense that we're understanding something that we're not understanding? The passage of time. We're in the swim, sinking in time, until finally we drown and go. This nonevent made into a great event while Consuela is here suffering the biggest event in her life. The Big Ending, though no one knows what, if anything, is ending and certainly no one knows what is beginning. It's a wild celebration of no one knows what.

Consuela alone knows, because Consuela now knows the wound of age. Getting old is unimaginable to anyone but the aging, but that is no longer so for Consuela. She no longer measures time like the young, marking backward to when you started. Time for the young is always made up of what is past, but for Consuela time is now how much future she has left, and she doesn't believe there is any. Now she measures time counting forward, counting time by the closeness of death. The illusion has been broken, the metronomic illusion, the comforting thought that, tick tock, everything happens in its proper time. Her sense of time is now the same as mine, speeded up and more forlorn even than mine. She, in fact, has overtaken me. Because I can still tell myself, "I'm not going to die in five years, maybe not in ten years, I'm fit, I'm well, I could even live another twenty," while she . . .

The loveliest fairy tale of childhood is that everything happens in order. Your grandparents go long before your parents, and your parents go long before you. If you're lucky it can work out that way, people aging and dying in order, so that at the funeral you ease your pain by thinking that the person had a long life. It hardly makes extinction less monstrous, that thought, but it's the trick that we use to keep the metronomic illusion intact and the time torture at bay: "So-and-so lived a long time." But Consuela has not been lucky, and so beside me she sits, under the sentence of death, while the nightlong merriment unfolds on the screen, a manufactured childish hysteria about embracing the open-ended future in ways that mature adults, with their melancholy knowledge of a very limited future, cannot have. And on this insane night, no one's knowledge can be more melancholy than hers.

"Havana," she says, and she weeps more forcefully by the moment, "I thought someday I will see Havana." "You will see Havana." "I won't. Oh, David, my grandfather . . ." "Yes, what about him? Go ahead, tell me, talk." "My grandfather would be sitting in the living room . . ." "Go on." I was holding her in my arms while she began to speak about herself as she never had before, never had cause to before, as, perhaps, she'd not even known herself before. "With *The NewsHour* on, with *The MacNeil-*

Lehrer NewsHour on, and," she said, through her copious tears, "he'd suddenly sigh, *'Pobre Mamá.'* Who'd died in Havana without him. Because their generation, that generation, did not leave. *'Pobre Mamá.' 'Pobre Papá.'* They stayed behind. He would just have this sadness, this longing for them. Terrible, terrible longing. And that's what I have. But it's for myself. It's for my life. I feel myself, I feel my body with my hands, I think, This is my body! It can't go away! This can't be real! This can't be happening! How can it go away? I don't want to die! David, I'm afraid to die!" "Consuela dear, you're not going to. You're thirty-two. You're not going to die for a very long time." "I grew up as an exile. So I'm scared of everything. Did you know that about me? *I'm scared of everything.*" "Oh, no. I don't think that's so. Of everything? It may seem so tonight but not—" "It's so *always*. I didn't want my family's exile. But you grow up and you hear 'Cuba, Cuba, Cuba' all the time . . . And look! Those people! Such vulgar people! Look what he has done to Cuba! I will never see it. I'll never see the house. I'll never see their house." "Yes, you will. Once Castro is gone—" "*I'll* be gone." "You won't be gone. You'll be here. Don't panic. There is no need to panic. You're going to be fine, you're going to live—" "You want to know the picture I've had? Of there? All my life? The picture in my head of Cuba?" "Yes. Tell me. Try to calm down and tell me everything. Do you want me to turn off the TV?" "No—no. They'll show something else. They *have* to." "Tell me the picture in your head, Consuela." "Not of the beach, not that. My parents had that. My parents talked about how much fun they had there, kids running around on the beach, people sitting in lounge chairs, ordering mimosas. They would take a house out on the beach and so on, but it wasn't that memory that I had. It was something else. I've had it forever. Oh, David— they buried Cuba long before they were buried. They had to. My father, my grandfather, my grandmother, they all knew they would never go back. And they never did. And now I never will." "You will," I told her. "What is the picture you've had forever? Talk to me. Talk," I said. "I always thought I would go back. Just to see the house. That it would be there." "Is the picture in your head of the house?" I asked her. "No. It's a road. El Malecón. If you see any kind of photos of Havana, you see a picture of El Malecón, this beautiful road right by the water. They've got this wall, and in the pictures everyone sits on the wall and hangs out. Did you see *Buena Vista Social Club*?" "I did. Because of you, of course

I did. I thought of you when I saw it." "Well, it's the road there," she said, "where the waves were crashing. That wall. You see it for just a moment. That's where I always thought I would be." "The road that might have been," I told her. "*Should* have been," Consuela said, and again she was weeping uncontrollably while up on the screen, beneath their lampshades (each, we learn, weighing fourteen pounds), the showgirls parade aimlessly across the stage. Yes, this is definitely Castro saying "Fuck you" to the twentieth century. Because it's the end of his adventure in history, too, of the mark he made and did not make on the score of human events. "Tell me," I said to her. "You never told me this before. You didn't talk like this eight years ago. Then you were a listener. My student. I never knew this. Go ahead. Tell me what should have been." "That wall," she said, "and me. That's all. Hanging out there and talking to people. That's it. You're by the water but you're in the city. It's a meeting spot. It's a promenade." "Well, it looked pretty rundown," I said, "in the movie." "It did. But that's not how I've seen it all my life."

And then the grief, then the weight of sadness for all that her family had lost, for her father and her grandparents dying in exile, for herself about to die in exile (and an exile she'd never before felt so cruelly), for all of the Castillos' Cuba that Castro had ruined, for everything she feared she was about to leave—all of it was so great that in my arms, for a full five minutes, Consuela went out of her mind. I saw, externalized, the terror that her body was feeling. "What is it? Consuela, what can I do for you? Tell me and I'll do it. What is it that's torturing you so?"

And here's what she told me when she was able to speak. Here, to my surprise, is what she told me tortured her most. "I always answered my parents in English. Oh, God. How I wish I had answered him more in Spanish." "Who?" "My father. He loved when I called him Papi. But after I was little, I never would. I called him Dad. I *had* to. I wanted to be an American. I did not want all their *sadness*." "Dearest Consuela, it doesn't matter now what you called him. He knew you loved him. He knew how much . . ." But there was no consoling her. I'd not heard her speak like this before, nor had I seen her behave as she did next, either. In every calm and reasonable person there is a hidden second person scared witless about death, but for someone thirty-two the time between Now and Then is ordinarily so vast, so boundless, that it's no more than maybe a couple of times a year, and then only for a moment or two and late at night, that one comes anywhere near encountering that second person and in the state of madness that is the second person's everyday life.

What she did then was to take off her hat. To throw off her hat. All this time, you see, she'd been wearing that fezlike hat, even when she was otherwise naked and I was taking the pictures of her breasts for her. But now she tore it off. With New Year's Eve abandon, tore off her funny New Year's Eve hat. First Castro's farce of a sexy stage show and now Consuela's mortality completely unveiled.

It was appalling to see her without the hat. A woman so young and beautiful with sort of feathery hair, very short, thin, colorless, meaningless hair—you'd rather have her bald after having been to the barber and been shaved than to see this idiotic fluff on her head. The transition from thinking of someone in the way you've always thought of that person—as just as alive as you are—to whatever signifies to you, as her fuzzy hairlessness did to me, that the person is close to death, is dying, I experienced at that moment not only as a shock but as a betrayal. A betrayal of Consuela for my having so rapidly absorbed the shock and made this accounting. The traumatic moment was upon us when the change occurs, when you discover that the other person's expectations can no longer resemble yours and that no matter how appropriately you may be acting and you may continue to act, he or she will leave before you do—if you're lucky, well before.

Itself. There it was. All the horror of it in that head. Consuela's head. I kissed it and kissed it. What else was there for me to do? The poison of the chemotherapy. All it had done to her body. All it had done to her mind. She's thirty-two, and she thinks she's now exiled from everything, experiencing each experience for the very last time. Only what if she isn't? What—

There! The phone! That could be—! At what time? It's two A.M. Excuse me!

It was. That was her. She called. Finally called. I have to leave. She is in a panic. She is having surgery in two weeks. She had her last chemotherapy. She asked me to tell her about the beauty of her body. That's why I was away so long. That's what she wanted to hear. That's what she's been talking about for nearly an hour. Her body. Do you think that after surgery a man will ever love my body again? This is what she asks again and again. You see, they've now decided to remove the entire breast. They were planning to go underneath the breast and to take a part of it. But now they think it's too serious for that. So they have to remove it. Ten weeks ago they told her they would remove only part of it, and now they tell her they are going to remove the whole thing. Mind you, this is a breast. It's not a small thing. This morning they told her what is going to happen; now it's night, and she's all alone and the whole prospect of everything . . . I have to go. She wants me there. She wants me to sleep in the bed with her there. She has not eaten all day. She has to eat. She has to be fed. You? Stay if you wish. If you want to stay, if you want to leave . . . Look, there's no time, I must run!

"Don't."

What?

"Don't go."

But I must. Someone has to be with her.

"She'll find someone."

She's in terror. I'm going.

"Think about it. Think. Because if you go, you're finished."

Philip Roth

I MARRIED A
COMMUNIST

'Knotted with energy, barely wasting a scene or a word in
its crackling velocity'
Mail on Sunday

Radio actor Iron Rinn is a big Newark roughneck blighted
by a brutal personal secret from which he is perpetually in
flight. An idealistic Communist, and uneducated ditchdigger
turned popular performer, a six-foot, six-inch Abe Lincoln
lookalike, he emerges from serving in WW2 passionately
committed to making the world a better place and winds up
instead blacklisted and unemployable, his life in ruins.

I Married a Communist is the story of Iron Rinn's denunciation
and disgrace. It is also the story of cruelty, humiliation,
betrayal and revenge – and American tragedy as only Philip
Roth can conceive one – fierce and funny, eloquently
rendered and deadly accurate.

'Roth remains as edgy, as furious, as funny, and as
dangerous as he was forty years ago'
New York Review of Books

Also available in Vintage

Philip Roth

OUR GANG

'The uncontested master of comic irony'
Time

In the character of Tricky – self-promoted legal whiz,
peace-loving Quaker – and, somehow, President of the
United States – Philip Roth has created one of contemporary
literature's greatest hypocritical opportunists.

An unprincipled self-seeker who hides his heartlessness
behind the anaesthetising clichés of high office, Tricky's
public language is a merciless parody o that 'candid'
Presidential prose which is merely double-talk.

Though steeped in fantasy and slapstick, *Our Gang* is
conceived in indignation, a satirical vision of a debased
national leadership speaking a language that, in Orwell's
words, 'is designed to make lies sound truthful an murder
respectable, and give an appearance of solidity to pure
wind'.

'A bitter yet hilarious lampoon... a remarkable display of
satiric vehemence. An extremely (in every sense) funny,
nail-bitingly anxious work'
Financial Times

VINTAGE

By Philip Roth
Also Available in Vintage

☐ Portnoy's Complaint	£6.99
☐ Our Gang	£6.99
☐ The Professor Of Desire	£6.99
☐ The Anatomy Lesson	£6.99
☐ The Prague Orgy	£6.99
☐ Zuckerman Bound	£6.99
☐ Deception	£6.99
☐ Patrimony	£6.99
☐ Sabbath's Theater	£6.99
☐ American Pastoral	£6.99
☐ I Married A Communist	£6.99

• All Vintage books are available through mail order or from your local bookshop.

• Payment may be made using Access, Visa, Mastercard, Diners Club, Switch and Amex, or cheque, eurocheque and postal order (sterling only).

☐☐☐☐☐☐☐☐☐☐☐☐☐☐☐☐

Expiry Date:_____ Signature:_____

Please allow £2.50 for post and packing for the first book and £1.00 per book thereafter.

ALL ORDERS TO:

Vintage Books, Books by Post, TBS Limited, The Book Service,
Colchester Road, Frating Green, Colchester, Essex, CO7 7DW, UK.
Telephone: (01206) 256 000
Fax: (01206) 255 914

NAME:_____

ADDRESS:_____

_____

_____

Please allow 28 days for delivery. Please tick box if you do not
wish to receive any additional information   ☐
Prices and availability subject to change without notice.